"I'm almost engaged to be married."

"Engaged?" So Mackenzie was spoken for. Why did Emma find that disappointing? He was a self-important, overbearing man's man, raised in an outpost where men were men and women were supposed to know their place.

"I...don't see why you're telling me this?"

"You're a grown woman, Emma. You know what's happening between us...."

"Perhaps you'd like to spell it out for me...."

"Physical attraction," Mackenzie said brutally. "Chemistry—something!"

ANN CHARLTON wanted to be a commercial artist but became a secretary. She wanted to play the piano but plays guitar instead, and she never planned to be a writer. From time to time she abseils, which surprises her because she is afraid of heights. Born in Sydney, Australia, Ann now lives in Brisbane. She would like to do more tapestry work and paint miniatures and has absolutely no plans to research a book in the Amazon or to learn to play the bouzouki.

Books by Ann Charlton

Don't miss any of our special offers. Write to us at the following address for information on our newest releases.

Harlequin Reader Service
U.S.: 3010 Walden Ave., P.O. Box 1325, Buffalo, NY 14269
Canadian: P.O. Box 609, Fort Erie, Ont. L2A 5X3

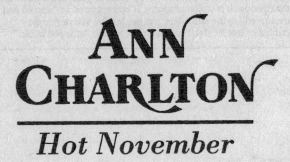

ANN CHARLTON

Hot November

Harlequin Books

TORONTO • NEW YORK • LONDON
AMSTERDAM • PARIS • SYDNEY • HAMBURG
STOCKHOLM • ATHENS • TOKYO • MILAN
MADRID • WARSAW • BUDAPEST • AUCKLAND

ISBN 0-373-11777-9

HOT NOVEMBER

First North American Publication 1995.

CHAPTER ONE

CATASTROPHE looked very like all the other country towns they had passed through. A broad main street, late Victorian shop-fronts and a central reservation planted optimistically with rose-bushes. The centenary celebrations had prompted the council to loop strings of multicoloured flags between the power poles. Every sixth flag was lime-green, Emma noticed, a scarce colour out here in the west where drought had coloured everything shades of red and ochre and dust. Heat shimmered, pressed down on corrugated roofs and into the spaces between. Only the flags moved, fluttering once in a sultry breath of air, before falling inert again. Emma, supervising the company's transfer from their two dusty vehicles into the Catastrophe pub, wondered if they had come to a ghost town.

In the pub, although there were smells of counter lunches and the sound of voices from the adjacent bar, the reception counter was deserted. A ceiling fan rotated indolently, stirring warm air. Emma set her bags down and found a bell, hidden behind a rack of postcards. She rang it as the others came in and the baggage piled up in the foyer. Bernie sniffed the air. His gourmet's nose wrinkled. 'Sausages,' he said drearily. 'And, if I'm not mistaken, steak, charred to a crisp. Served with shovelfuls of *chips* and dollops of tomato sauce from horrible little packets. Lord, Emma—I suppose we must sleep here, but will we have to *eat* here, too?'

Emma cursed his splendid actor's voice. Was it her imagination or had the conversation stopped in the bar?

'What a dump,' Alison said, her voice as carrying as Bernie's.

'I think it's charming,' Emma countered desperately, dragging her eyes from a row of very green, very plastic potted palms. She put a finger to her lips and pointed at the open door but none of them took any notice. Alison blew cigarette smoke at the collection of clumsy amateur paintings that covered the walls. Price tags were attached to each and a sign over them announced 'Art for Sale, by J. Clements'. 'Art for sale? J. Clements should be shot for calling this art,' Alison hooted.

They grouped around the paintings, Reg joining in as Alison and Bernie loosed their acid wit on the unfortunate J. Clements. A firing squad of three. Their tempers were frayed from three weeks of travelling on country roads, performing to half-filled houses, sleeping in motels and pubs. Her crew were just waiting for a legitimate excuse to break their contracts and ditch the whole project. Emma selected a postcard, mindful that her best friend would expect another update of the tour. 'Dear Ami,' she thought, composing in her mind. 'Heat, dust and flies. A burst tyre and one shattered windscreen last week. Yesterday, I hit a kangaroo on the road. Today I might murder my crew. Wish you were here.'

Nobody came and Emma went through to the bar. Six or seven men stopped talking as she entered. Six or seven pairs of eyes followed her. Emma was taller than average, more statuesque than she liked, and had thick, blonde hair that she wore in a single braid more often than not. 'The grey-eyed, voluptuous Ms Spencer', a sour theatre reviewer had described her once. She was used to being looked at, but so many fixed stares made her wonder if her shirt buttons had sprung open. Into the silence came Bernie's voice, clear as a bell through the doorway. 'Darling, be fair—what would you expect in a hick town—undiscovered Van Goghs in the pub?'

Emma cringed but there was nothing to do but pretend she hadn't heard. To the man behind the bar she said, 'Is there someone who can book us into the hotel? We have a reservation.'

But the bartender was out from behind the counter, making little shooing motions at her. Almost, Emma thought, as if he were trying to discourage a cow that had wandered into the wrong paddock. 'Be with you in two ticks, blossom,' he said, his body language saying loud and clear that this territory was unofficially reserved for bulls only. *Blossom.* If she weren't so tired, she would sit down and order a drink just for the hell of it. But she left, unequal to the task of insisting upon equality.

It was several ticks of the clock before the man came through, introduced himself with a leisurely air as Col Mundy and crowned Emma's awful day with disastrous news.

'What do you mean, there's no reservation?' she repeated. Suspiciously she eyed him, wondering if he was exacting revenge for their cracks about his cuisine, décor and artwork. 'There must be one for us—the Shoelace Theatre. Five single rooms for ten days. I'm Emma Spencer, the theatre director—perhaps the booking is in my name?'

Col moved with the same exasperating slowness as his ceiling fan. 'Nope,' he said at last.

'But we're here for the town's centenary celebrations. I'm directing the showground display for the opening ceremony——'

Col showed a flicker of interest. 'Yeah, my eldest girl's been practising for that—marching about with coloured pom-poms. Could be a bit of a flop, I reckon.'

Emma hardily assured him it would be all right on the day, she'd done this kind of thing before. 'But we're doing our comedy this week—at the community hall—and the Forrest Commemorative performance at the amphitheatre to wind up your festival next week, so you see——'

'Yeah. I've got tickets to the comedy. I like a good laugh.' He looked dourly at Emma, challenging her and her players to make him laugh.

On cue came derisive laughter from her players. 'Your centenary committee chairman was attending to our accommodation as part of the deal.'

'Ah. There's your problem, then. Roy Jackson had to go off suddenly to his daughter in Perth. Must have forgotten to book you in.'

'Well, can we have rooms anyway?'

Emma waited. The ceiling fan turned and Col flicked pages. 'Sorry. I'm all full up what with folks coming in for the celebrations. I reckon the motel is all booked out, too. You'd better talk to the Boss. Roy handed everything over to the Boss.'

'Who is the Boss?' she asked wearily. And boss of what?

'Boss Mackenzie,' Col said on a note of surprise, as if the man was such a giant that he was surely known as far away as Sydney. The Boss, Col said, was salt of the earth, a real good sport. He had his own place out of town a bit, was president of a graziers' association, a councillor with an office in town and head honcho of the volunteer fire brigade. Boss of just about everything, apparently.

'I'll go and see your Mr Mackenzie, then. What's his first name?'

'Just call him "Boss",' Col told her with a gravedigger's smile. 'Most everyone does.'

Emma just knew what this Mackenzie would be like. One of the sunburned, paunchy types who got carried away with being master of all they surveyed on their cattle and sheep stations and felt the need to run everything else as well. He would be in his element with big groups of men and believe that women belonged in the kitchen or the maternity ward. He would be tolerant, avuncular and patronising, call her 'girlie' or 'love' or 'blossom' and pity her for her single status. 'But don't you worry, love,' one big, bluff grazier had consoled her during one country town stopover. 'You're a good-looking woman and a sensible man is bound to snap you up any minute.' As if she was a sardine that had so far failed to attract a cruising shark. Emma had smiled and denied herself the pleasure of telling him that, at twenty-eight, she considered herself yet to reach her prime and had no intention of being snapped up again. One escape from a cruising shark was enough for any sensible woman.

'Anyway, you've got no hope of seeing Mackenzie today,' Col said, with a perverse pride that their local bigwigs were not readily available to outsiders. 'He's out alongside the school, burning a fire-break. There's been a nasty outbreak of fires the last fortnight. You probably passed some on your way here.'

Impatiently, Emma said they hadn't. 'When would he be likely to finish with this fire-break?'

'He'll be there all day. All night too, I reckon, if a wind gets up.' He looked beyond her to the paintings, still the focus of attention. 'Nice of your lot to take such an interest,' he said blandly. 'A local painted them. Very well known around these parts.' He closed the register with a permanent little snap. Emma gritted her teeth and bought the postcard for Ami, to show that she had no hard feelings.

An hour and a half later Emma was hot, tired and full of hard feelings. She had been to Councillor Mackenzie's office and been redirected to Councillor Jackson's office without any results. The town's two boarding houses, one motel and block of rental apartments were all booked out for the festival. What was more, Emma discovered a growing coolness on the part of the locals she spoke to. In desperation, she rang

the man Mackenzie's mobile phone number, hoping to
catch him at the fire site. At length a laconic voice
answered and, doing some fast talking, Emma pre-
vailed upon the man to take a message to Mackenzie.
'I'll hold on for his answer,' she said firmly.

If she'd thought things moved in slow-motion before,
now she wondered if all activity had ceased. Fifteen
minutes later, when she was almost expiring in a
suffocating phone booth, he returned to tell her that
the Boss would be in his town office at seven-thirty if
she wanted to see him.

'But that's too late——' she said.

'Well, sorry, love. But he's got work to do and that's
the way of it.'

He hung up. Emma crashed the receiver down. 'And
I've got work to do too, *Boss*!' she muttered. Reso-
lutely, she went back to the pub and into the public bar
where a new shift of drinkers checked out her shirt
buttons. She slid a town map in front of a scandalised
Col, whose hands just naturally started with the
'shooing' motions.

'I want to get to the school, Col,' she appealed, and
allowed her eyelashes the faintest flutter. 'And I don't
want to take a wrong turn.'

Faced with a map and a female in distress, Col rose
to the occasion before he realised it. 'But you don't
want to go running out *there*, love,' he said, as if she'd
announced she was off to a remote Amazon jungle
with nothing but her handbag. 'A fire-site's no place
for a woman at any time and this is the hottest
November we've had for sixty years,' he said with
proud pessimism.

Emma reflected that a fire-site in the hottest
November for half a century was probably no place for
a man, either.

'Besides, Boss Mackenzie doesn't like women getting
mixed up with burn-offs.'

'Well, I suppose it's an improvement on the days when women were essential at burn-offs,' she said drily, folding up the map to stow it in her bag. Smiling at his puzzlement, she explained, 'Witch-burning. A nasty, outmoded form of chauvinism.'

She saw the smoke long before she saw the fire. Catastrophe Primary School looked deserted so presumably the children had been sent home early to escape the smoke. Emma turned off the main road onto a dirt track and moments later came upon a bushfire brigade tanker, a motorbike and a collection of vehicles. They were set well back from the lighted grass in a large section of open forest. Several men, wearing helmets and using hand radios, stood at intervals along a ploughed strip of ground. Emma parked alongside the motorbike and got out of the van.

Some of the area had already been extensively burned and the blackened ground steamed gently in the sun. There were two fires burning towards each other in ragged lines through the tall trees and sapling growth. Long blades of dry grass shrivelled, twigs and leaf litter glowed and disintegrated. Emma looked in vain for a touch of green. There was only umber and ochre and a lifeless olive brown and, after the flames had passed, nothing but a depressing black.

Men in knee-high boots with water back-packs and hoses trudged along behind the lines of fire, putting out any lingering sparks. Other men stood about, hands on hips or leaning on trees, talking into hand radios and drinking from tin water flasks. The air was hazed with smoke, stinging her eyes. The sound of the fire was a subtle, low note beneath the spit and crackle.

'Beautiful, isn't she?' a voice said in her ear.

Emma turned. She was used to good-looking men but standing beside her, oddly elegant in overalls and helmet, was a man to inspire poetry. Dark blue eyes, wildly curling dark hair, tanned skin, full mouth and flashing, perfect teeth.

Emma tried not to gape. 'Sorry?'

'The fire,' he explained.

'It was the *she* that threw me,' she said wryly. 'Surely a fire is an *it*?'

He grinned. 'Just a figure of speech.' He wiped his hand across his overalls, then extended it. 'I'm Steve Mackenzie.'

Emma blinked. He was a boy, twenty-two or three at the most. '*You're* Boss Mackenzie?'

'That would strain the imagination, wouldn't it?' he said lightly, but his mouth had turned sulky. 'You want the *other* Mackenzie.' He pointed to a figure within shouting distance. 'My big brother. Not much family resemblance, is there?' he said, and she couldn't tell if he was glad or sorry about it, which was odd because even from here she could see that the other Mackenzie didn't share his extraordinary looks.

The 'Boss' nickname was no joke. There was authority in the way he stood, in the tilt of his head as he spoke into a hand radio and in the confidence of slow-motion semaphore commands. He was neither the paunchy type she'd expected nor anything like the younger Mackenzie. He was taller, bigger in the shoulders. Endurance sprang to mind, rather than elegance.

Emma mentally girded herself and started toward him. Steve took her arm and said, 'Um—better stay here. Visitors can't go any closer. Boss's orders. I'll let him know you're waiting.'

So she curbed her impatience and waited and watched as Steve pointed her out to the boss. The older Mackenzie looked around without surprise. If he'd seen her arrive, her identity as one of the theatre company was no secret. The van was splashed with slogans advertising the theatre and Catastrophe's centenary. 'We're on our way to Catastrophe' was the slogan she'd chosen against all advice from more superstitious colleagues. Emma had regretted it a hundred times since.

Suddenly she became the focus of all eyes. When the Boss looked at something, everyone looked, apparently. Emma leaned against the van, her hair tucked up under a cap, glad of her sunglasses which gave her some illusion of privacy.

Minutes passed. The boss directed Steve to take up a new position and, as he went, the boy looked over at her with an eloquent shrug. Instead of coming to her, Mackenzie turned away in the opposite direction.

Emma straightened. 'Hey!' she called. 'Mr Mackenzie!'

He didn't bat an eye. Her raised voice had drawn all eyes to her again and she set off after Mackenzie conscious of her audience. 'Hello!' she yelled. 'I need to talk to you——'

A man stepped in front of her. 'Sorry, lady, you can't go any further without a helmet. Safety precautions.'

That was not so bad, but he wriggled his fingertips at her in a motion that was reminiscent of Col shooing the cows from the paddock. 'Well, how about finding me a spare helmet?' she said reasonably.

'Can't do that, love. You just hang about, he'll be back in a while.'

'Where's he going?' she asked as Mackenzie stepped up on to the tractor and was carried slowly but relentlessly further away.

'Probably around to the other side of the site.'

'How long will that take?'

'Oh, jeez—half an hour, an hour, maybe.'

Astonished, Emma put her hands on her hips. 'I can't wait around an *hour* before I even get to speak to him! It will only take a few minutes. Surely he could

speak to me first? It isn't as if any of you are exactly in
a rush!' she said, indicating the snail-pace of the
tractor, the almost pastoral air of the scene with men
leaning about, brushing away flies. The two lines of fire
had consumed all the fuel in their path and had fizzled
out upon meeting. 'You're not exactly flat out fighting
an inferno.'

The tractor pulled in and idled, but only so that the
two men could consult a large chart. Emma strode
along, parallel to the forbidden territory. 'Mr
Mackenzie!' she yelled, but neither the driver nor
Mackenzie looked up. 'Hey!' she shouted, in frustration, aware that the man's rules and regulations had
conveniently put him out of her reach. He could
pretend she wasn't there and there was nothing she
could do about it.

'Take it easy, darl. He can't hear you,' another man
said, admiring her legs. He exchanged a comment with
a colleague that brought a shared leer at Emma and a
guffaw of laughter. Someone else wolf-whistled.
Unwanted attention galore, she thought, fulminating.

'We'll see about that, *darl*,' she muttered, marching
back to the van to fling open the back doors of the van.
She uncovered the audio equipment, plugged in the
leads and hooked up the power pack. The speakers
were on the roof-rack, and she climbed up, threw off
the protective covers and dragged up the leads to
connect them. Then she snapped in a microphone on a
long wire, turned the amplification sky-high and
hitched herself up on to the back bumper, steadying
herself against the roof-rack.

'Hello, Mr Mackenzie,' she said into the mike. His
name echoed. Mackenzie. . . Mackenzie. There was a
sudden, gratifying activity. Men bolted upright from
tree trunks, spilled water from flasks, came running
out from the bush. 'My name is Emma Spencer——'
she said, speaking slowly to allow for distortion.

Emma. . . Emma. Spencer. . . Spencer. 'I would be most grateful for a few minutes of your time.'

The men were gazing at her in amazement now and, after the run-around she'd had, that was gratifying too. Always mindful of the dwindling profit margin of the tour, Emma felt she couldn't waste this captive audience. 'While I'm waiting, may I remind you all that we'll be performing a little ripper of a comedy at the community hall tomorrow and Saturday night. If you haven't got your tickets, there will be some available at the door. Stay to meet the cast for refreshments afterwards   and   help   your   local   charity organisations——'

With satisfaction she switched off. Of course, this was no way to open up negotiations with the Mackenzie man, but how could things get any worse, anyway? It was a liberating thought and a timely one. A burly figure got down from the tractor. This time, he was coming in her direction and at a spanking pace, the fastest thing she'd seen on two legs since hitting Catastrophe. In a place committed to slow motion it could only be a bad omen.

With the calm and efficiency of practice, she returned her equipment to its precise space in the van, slammed the doors and dusted off her hands on the back of her shorts. As Mackenzie steamed up to her, her surge of satisfaction was followed by a mighty surge of adrenalin. This was a big, tough-looking man, an ugly customer in every sense of the word. He wore a shirt with the collar turned up, and trousers made of some heavy fire-retardant fabric supported by braces and tucked into boots. A pair of gauntlets were stuffed into a broad black belt, with a hand radio and a holstered knife. He was smeared with dust and charcoal, gleaming with sweat. Craggy features, bloodshot eyes with pounches underneath, a blunt chin bristling with vigorous growth. More like Steve's father than his brother. Very likely he was grey or balding under that safety helmet. Emma held on to the thought of thinning hair in the face of this excessive masculinity.

'Mr Mackenzie?' she said politely, as if she hadn't bawled his name over the countryside to summon him. 'I'm Emma Spencer.'

'I heard.' Dry as dust.

She laughed. 'Yes, well, I did bump the amps up. I wanted to catch you before you got too far away.'

'Well—you *caught* me,' he said.

And he was too big to throw back. 'Nice to meet you,' she said, tongue-in-cheek and extended her hand. He glanced down at it but kept both his hands low on his hips in the bossman pose. Emma stood there, conscious of the ground being cut from under her with this most masculine of rebuffs.

'You won't hold a grudge, will you, Mr Mackenzie?' she asked with her most dazzling smile. 'I hear you're a good sport.'

But the good sport kept his hands on his hips. Emma withdrew her hand, trying to look nonchalant about it. The heat from the scorched earth and the sun seemed suddenly more intense.

'A few minutes of my time, you said, Miss Spencer.'

'You got my message, Mr Mackenzie, so you know the problem that has come up with our accommo- dation——'

'And you got mine. I told you I will be in my office at seven-thirty tonight.'

'Seven-thirty,' she said evenly, 'will be much too late.'

'I can do nothing for you before then. As you might have noticed, I am supervising a controlled burn.'

'I am not asking you to do me a *favour*,' she said sharply. 'I am asking you to take some responsibility for a mistake made by your committee.'

His head tipped back and he looked down his nose

at her. His nostrils gently flared. 'I don't know anything about the matter at this point,' he said.

'You must know something! We must be booked in somewhere under another name—maybe one of the committee's names. Roy Jackson's secretary said you have the files——'

'But not on my person.' He moved his hands wide of his body as if inviting her to do a body search. She must have made some small backward move, for Mackenzie's mouth quirked as he scored a cheap point. One of his men guffawed.

'Could you at least suggest some alternatives?' she said coolly. 'I know you are busy, Mr Mackenzie. I am busy too. We've driven a long way this morning. I have a stage set to unload and assemble this afternoon and a very tiring technical rehearsal to direct. I need to settle the accommodation question before, not after a day's work.'

There did seem to be a spark of empathy at last. But by the time the radio had crackled and he'd yanked out the aerial and barked some answer into it, any trace of it had vanished.

'Look, I have to go. Meet me at my office, and I dare say I can do something for you,' he said.

This continued insistence that he might do her a favour rankled. 'Why not now? You're a local, you know people. You could phone someone from your car.'

But forgive and forget did not appear to be part of his philosophy. Mackenzie gave her a hard look that said she might have brought him running, but he didn't take orders, he gave them. 'Miss Spencer, this is a fire site and I can't guarantee your safety. So why don't you go back to town, fix up your stage set, practise your lines and have a cup of tea or whatever actors like to drink. I'll be in my office tonight and I'll do what I can to help you then.' He strode off. Emma gaped. He

might as well have patted her on the head and told her
to run away and play while the grown-ups got on with
their work. *Whatever actors liked to drink.* Maybe he
thought theatre people were all booze-artists. She took
off after him.

'What is this magic about your office? You can't
spare me a few minutes *here* but tonight, in your office,
when it's too late, you can move the earth for me?'

He stopped. 'I never promised to move the earth for
you, Miss Spencer,' he said gravely. 'I hardly know
you,'

Hilarious. Emma heard one of his men snigger. He
set off again and she went after him, viewing his big,
sweaty back and beefy shoulders. He turned to look
hard at her and her nerves jumped.

'We're going to have to work together at some time
over the next week, so why don't you call me Emma?
What do I call you?' she said amicably. 'I'm afraid I
draw the line at "Boss".' She smiled and took off her
sunglasses as a gesture toward more friendly relations.
He refused this one too, his eyes narrowed.

'Just Mackenzie will do.'

'OK, Mackenzie,' she said, taking him literally. She
kept pace with him as he detailed some men to burn
off several small sections that had escaped the flames.
Nothing was to be left alive in one of the boss's burns,
Emma thought, wistfully enjoying a touch of green in
a surviving clump of wild flowers. Eventually he
noticed she was still with him and stopped, looking
exasperated. His gaze flickered over her face and
briefly downward. Emma began to wonder about her
shirt buttons again when he suddenly looked away and
rubbed at his smarting eyes.

'You said you'd tried Roy's office?' he said, staring
off at some far horizon.

As an olive branch it was more like a twig, but she
grabbed it. Eagerly, she filled him in on her efforts to

sort the problem out. 'If I could have got some information, I wouldn't be here,' she explained. 'Nobody seemed to know anything, or if they did, they weren't telling me.'

A pause. Emma forced herself to wait.

'We're a small community. Word travels fast. You and your crew have very—*carrying* voices.' This last with an ironic glance at the speakers on top of the van.

His own voice was unexpectedly good. Untrained, of course, and with the pronounced drawl of the country, but deep with a suggestion of roughness in the timbre. *Word travels fast.* 'What? You don't mean the things they—we—said in the pub? About the sausages and chips? J. Clements' paintings?'

At his nod, she groaned, took off her cap and wiped her brow with the back of her hand. Her plait fell down and absently she twitched it over her shoulder. Its sudden appearance seemed to distract him. 'We didn't intend to hurt anyone's feelings, Mackenzie. I apologise. What can we do to redeem ourselves?'

He smiled nastily. 'Worried the country *hicks* might retaliate by not buying tickets to your play?'

'Darned right!'

A snort of a laugh. 'That's honest at least.'

'Except I wouldn't have used the word "hicks".'

'That's not what I heard.'

He was gone again, setting a pace that was surely against the law in Catastrophe, and doggedly she followed. 'Have you got the hotel *bugged*?' she said to his back. If only the damned man would stand *still*. 'Look——' she began, and was drowned out by the roar of the tractor as it turned. 'Look, Mackenzie——' she started again when her foot rolled on a twig and sent her sprawling. He grabbed her arm, hauled her up efficiently so that she came face to face with him. This close, the shadow on his jaw resolved into individual bristles. He had the same classical straight nose as his

brother but none of the generous curves of lips and
brows. Mackenzie's mouth was lopsided, thinner-
lipped, his brows thick and straight, and his eyes were
squinted so hard together as to be invisible. He might
have warm blue eyes like his brother but she wouldn't
bank on it. Perspiration had driven the dust and
charcoal into the lines around his eyes and mouth,
marking them sharply as if drawn in ink. He smelled of
smoke and sweat. His grip bit into her arm and she was
uncomfortably conscious of the size and strength of his
hand. On the whole, Emma thought, she would have
preferred to fall flat on her face. The heat was worse
than ever and she slapped her cap back on her head
with a flourish. The brim grazed his forehead and his
eyes widened as he tipped his head out of the way.

'You've got green eyes,' she said in surprise.

He was taken aback. 'What?'

'Green eyes. It's unusual.'

A long pause. '*You're* unusual,' he said at last.

'And that's not meant to be a compliment, is it?'

'Did you expect a compliment in return?'

'What makes you think I was complimenting you?
Maybe I don't *like* green eyes.'

He smiled then, showing very white, even teeth that
had worn better than the rest of him. When he let her
go, Emma stepped back, relieved to restore a proper
space between them but conscious of a flicker of
interest in Mackenzie the man.

'I could arrange for some sleeping bags,' he said
diffidently. 'I can give you permission to sleep overnight in the community hall.'

'Sleeping bags on the *floor*?' she said, astounded.
'Why not just give me an axe and tell me to hew a
shelter out of the wilderness?'

His shoulders shook in amusement. He turned away
to make a big John Wayne gesture to which the tractor
responded with a roar. Emma eyed its advance sus-

piciously, wondering if he'd somehow given the signal for her to be forcibly removed.

'Well, I certainly have to hold out for a better offer than sleeping bags,' she said.

'We could accommodate you at the campgrounds, I suppose.'

'Tents? Is that a better offer?' She shook her head. 'Can we get serious about this? Your committee has a contract with the theatre and I have a contract with my crew. If they are not accommodated as per that contract, they will walk out.'

'Then I suggest that might be a leadership problem, Miss Spencer,' he said. 'No crew of mine would walk out on purely legal grounds. They'd show a little loyalty.'

The man was definitely trying to needle her. But it caught Emma on the raw. For the first time in years, one of her pet projects had gone sour and the sense of failure went deep.

'You must tell me the secret of your success some time,' she said tartly, annoyed that she'd found him interesting even for a moment. 'For now, I require proper bedrooms with bathrooms and breakfast included.'

Mackenzie took off his safety helmet and ran a large, dirty hand over his head. His hair was dark brown, dead straight and thick as fur. Such plenitude made a mockery of her prediction of greyness or baldness. Emma was reminded of a grizzly bear she'd seen in a zoo, except that the grizzly had been more appealing. 'Miss Spencer,' he said, as to a troublesome, dim child. 'We are suffering drought conditions. This is our hottest November in sixty years. The fire hazard is extreme. Over the next week hundreds of people will visit our town—some of them careless people who will toss cigarettes and half-extinguished matches out of car windows and light campfires against all prohibitions. I

am engaged in burning firebreaks to protect our town-
ship. It *grieves* me that four actors from the city might
have to spend even one night without every modern
convenience, it really does.' He held his helmet over
his heart, playing to the gallery, and there was a spatter
of laughter from his men. Perhaps they were so loyal
they laughed at all his witticisms. 'But this is more
important and you'll have to wait. Either you go to the
campgrounds, or see me this evening. Seven-thirty. My
office.'

He put on the helmet again and went. Emma glared
at his back, recognising a lost cause. As she climbed up
on the van to cover the speakers and check the load
straps, one of the men wolf-whistled at her bare legs
and yelled that he'd give her a bed for the night and
other benefits into the bargain. More grins and guffaws.
The sound brought Mackenzie's head around and he
said something sharply to the man. Perhaps when he
said he couldn't guarantee her safety, he hadn't been
talking about the fire hazard. She slammed the door so
hard that the van rocked.

She was overtaken by a motorbike on the way back
to town. The rider flagged her down. Behind the
helmet she recognised Steve Mackenzie. She pulled
over and as Steve flipped up his visor and bent to her
window with a dazzling smile, she said coolly, 'This
had better be good. Mackenzies are not my favourite
fruit right now.'

Steve laughed. 'Hey, I can't help being related to the
Boss man.' He pulled a pen and a scrap of paper from
his overalls and jotted something down. 'This is Sara
Hardy's address. She's the president of the local drama
club. She was expecting guests for the centenary but I
heard this morning that they've cancelled. Her nose is
out of joint because the committee drafted in you
professionals for the centenary finale instead of using

her group, but I think she might help you out for one night.'

Emma was beginning to wonder if there was anyone in this town who didn't hold a grudge against them.

'There's a catch. She's written a play,' he said, grinning. 'You might have to offer to read it.'

She sighed. 'If that's the price, I'll pay it. Why are you being helpful? Your brother might be annoyed. He seems to think a tent is more than we deserve.'

'Helping you is a pleasure, Emma. Annoying Matt is a bonus,' he said with a grin and, turning his bike, roared away with a bravura one-wheel start.

Matt. Way ahead, the hot road surface appeared to turn to water in a shimmering heat mirage. Matt Mackenzie. '"I never promised to move the earth for you,",' she mimicked, clenching the steering-wheel. Awful man. All grit and bristles and no manners. But eyes the colour of deep water and a voice to raise the hair on the back of your neck. She thought about this grudgingly, wanting to deny him any saving grace. A voice to raise the hackles, more like.

Sara Hardy overcame her resentment and offered her own perfectly decorated house for the night. 'But I already have someone staying so I can only take three,' she said, even after Emma had offered to read her script. Glad to avert a mutiny from her crew, Emma accepted. When she left, with Sara's manuscript under her arm, the smell of roast beef was in the air and feather pillows were being encased in crisp lawn ready for her crew. She thought of these comforts wistfully later, as she suffered heartburn from an indifferent hamburger from a snack bar and resigned herself to sleeping in the van. Or, as it turned out, to insomnia in the van.

The question of where to park the van was determined by her appointment with Mackenzie at his office. He didn't turn up at seven-thirty and stubbornly, she

stayed on in his office parking space long after it was
clear he had no intention of coming. One place was as
good as another in a strange town.

She turned on the interior light and wrote on the
postcard for Ami. 'The boss man in Catastrophe is a
real MCP with Adonis for a brother. I must be mad,
touring in summer. This is the hottest November here
for sixty years! The things I do for an Arts Council
grant. This morning I hit a kangaroo on the road. I feel
like a murderer. Wish I were there.' She stuck a stamp
on the postcard. Ami would want to know all about
the Adonis when she got back. She imagined herself
describing Steve Mackenzie over coffee in Ami's shop
and suffered a wave of homesickness. The tour was a
disaster any way you looked at it.

From habit Emma felt in her pocket for her lucky
charm. Simon had given it to her, which was bad luck,
but she hadn't known that at the time. After he'd gone,
she'd almost tossed the gold cigarette lighter in the
wastebin along with the other Simon memorabilia.
Instead, she had kept it to remind her never to surren-
der control of her own life again. It had worked. She
tossed the lighter in her hand and rubbed her thumb
over the engraved message. 'To Emma, who lights up
my life. Simon.' The inscription could still deliver a
string after nearly four years. Seemingly simple, sincere
words. Emma flicked the mechanism and watched the
flame. But there had been nothing simple about Simon.

Time passed. Emma drifted into a twilight zone, not
sleeping, not awake. Her sleep-starved mind chose the
kangaroo incident to play and replay. She felt again
the terrible thud of motor-driven metal as it hit a living
animal, the vibration that travelled through the vehicle
and into her hands on the steering-wheel. The moment
of truth, when she got out dreading the sight of the
dead creature. The first thing she'd ever killed. Every
time she closed her eyes, the same scene unfolded until

at last her mind offered her a variation and it was Mackenzie instead of the kangaroo lying there, his grizzly brown hair and bristling jaw streaked with blood. She let out a cry and thrashed around, rocking the van, hearing the thud of a car door nearby.

Footsteps came close to the van, circled it. Heart pounding, Emma reached for the lock. Too late. The van door swung open and the interior light went on. A man bent to look inside. Big, sloping shoulders filled the door space. Two large hands grasped the door-frame. The Boss man himself.

She stared at him. 'I thought you were dead,' she said.

CHAPTER TWO

'WISHFUL thinking?' Mackenzie said.

'Instead of the kangaroo.'

He looked thoughtfully at her, then around the van's interior. 'Are you alone? Or are your pals picketing the back entrance to my office as well?'

Emma surfaced more fully from her exhausted twilight.

'My *crew* is sleeping off roast beef on feather pillows at Sara Hardy's place, thanks to Steve. He had the decency to come after me with the address and an introduction.'

'So that's where he went this time. He didn't mention his good deed,' he said sarcastically. 'But you're sleeping outside my office—as a protest, or what?'

'I'm using your parking space but no one could accuse me of *sleeping* here. Sleeping is not something I do well, even with a sprung mattress and feather pillow,' she said, feeling a certain fixedness in her focus. She closed her eyes momentarily to stop staring at him. 'Sara would only take three of us. I would have slept on the floor but she doesn't like bodies messing up her interior design.' Remembering the sensitivities of Catastrophe people, Emma held up a hand. 'Not that I'm complaining, Mackenzie. I don't like *my* house in a mess, either. She offered my people hospitality and I wasn't about to hang around making her feel guilty in case I spoiled it for everyone else, that's all.'

'You're rambling,' he observed.

'You're *late*.'

'You surely got my message that I couldn't make it back by seven-thirty?'

'How did you send it?' she enquired, piqued at his commanding tone. 'I *did* see a pigeon fly over a while back, but it didn't stop.'

His mouth tightened. 'I asked one of the men to stop by to tell you that I would be late, to go to the campgrounds.'

'Well, he didn't.'

'Damn!'

Was it the fact that she'd been inconvenienced that annoyed him? More likely that someone hadn't obeyed his orders. 'Is it a leadership problem, do you think, Mackenzie?' she mocked, reminding him of the lofty criticism that had stung her pride. But she was too tired and, though she disliked him, she couldn't recover the intensity of her former anger. He was smeared with dirt, ash flecked the chest hair visible in the V of his drill shirt, his eyes were red and his stubble pronounced. 'You look even worse than before,' she said as a statement of fact, without malice, knowing she looked similarly strained. She was grubby from the exertions of setting up the stage, wrung out from the frustrating technical rehearsal with the hall's very basic system.

'I dare say,' he said, letting his head drop. His chest heaved and he stood there, arms spanning the open door. Two in the morning and he was still wearing the same clothes so he must have only just finished with the firebreak. 'What happened.' she asked. 'Did the wind change?'

'Just before midnight. We finished the burn shortly after you were there. I stayed on patrol until the wind dropped again.' He seemed belatedly surprised that she would enquire.

'Alone?' she asked.

He nodded. Emma grimaced. 'Being the boss has its disadvantages. Your crew and mine are tucked up in bed, but you and I haven't even had a shower.'

Mackenzie looked a bit quizzical at this and she realised that she could have phrased it less intimately. Too weary to care, she waved a hand. 'Why aren't you home getting a hot shower, Mackenzie?' she asked. 'I presume you didn't drop by to do some paperwork?'

He seemed to come to a decision and held the door wide. Keys jingled in his hand. 'You'd better come into my office, Miss Spencer.'

'Why? I don't take shorthand,' she quipped.

No smile quirked his harsh mouth. No sense of humour, Emma thought. Surprise, surprise.

'My place is well over an hour from town so I often stay here overnight when I'm working late on council business. Bring in a change of clothes if you want. You can use my shower.'

Emma sat up straight. 'A shower,' she repeated in a reverent tone.

'And towels.'

She felt an almost grovelling gratitude at the thought and she sprang from the van on a wave of unsuspected energy. He stepped out of her way, watched as she opened the back doors of the van and felt around for her overnight bag.

'I almost didn't come back here tonight,' he said, as if he was thinking out loud. He passed a hand wearily over his face. 'I dare say I wouldn't have, if I'd known you were here, lying in wait for me. The woman I least want to run into. . .'

Emma snorted at this image of herself as huntress, waiting to pounce on a man more than equipped to take care of himself. 'I'm not exactly planning to write you into my memoirs either, Mackenzie. At least, I wasn't, until you offered me a shower.'

She heard him laugh as he moved away to unlock his office. By the time she had found her overnight bag he had gone inside, leaving the door open. A mellow light appeared in the front office window. She went through the smoked glass door labelled 'Matthew B. Mackenzie, Councillor.' This was a man to whom the people of Catastrophe brought their grievances, she marvelled. A local champion of rights!

His office, seen earlier, looked cosier by night. Two desks, one with a large, swivel chair, one with a word-processor. Crammed bookshelves and file cabinets and a three-seater divan that looked a trifle short for Mackenzie's sleepovers. Only a desk lamp was switched on. There was no sign of Mackenzie but she heard the shower just a few seconds before it turned off. Emma looked at his books and journals, an assortment on public administration, agriculture and meteorology. A town map and some old sepia photo-graphs of Catastrophe in various stages of natural disasters and subsequent rebuilding hung on the walls. Had the town's name come first and the floods and bushfires later, or the other way around? she won-dered. Alongside was a painting, also of the town, with a distorted perspective to the main street that looked familiar. Fatalistically, she peered at the signature. Emma groaned. Who else but the popular J. Clements?

Behind the larger desk, leaning against the wall, was a map chart of the regional area. Emma picked it up and ran a finger along the route the company had taken on the way to Catastrophe. Red stickers were placed against a number of towns she remembered with a certain dreariness. The bathroom door opened and Mackenzie came up behind her.

'Do the red dots represent us, Mackenzie? Have you been mapping our progress, just *waiting* to roll out the red carpet for us?' she said, tongue-in-cheek. He reached over her shoulder and took the chart, giving her a cool look that made her feel like a snoop. 'It was just sitting there in full view,' she protested.

Her voice trailed off as she got a good look at him. He was practically naked. A royal blue towel was

wrapped around his waist. His hair was wet and had
been slicked back with a large-toothed comb. He still
needed a shave and there were bags under his eyes,
but now that the grime had been washed from the
grooves in his face he looked younger. Not good-
looking, just not quite so rough. Mackenzie frowned
down at the chart. 'What do you mean—mapping your
progress?' he asked, turning the map to the light. His
substantial muscles rippled with the movement. Drop-
lets of water glistened with fairy-like daintiness on iron-
hard biceps and in the spattering of dark hair on his
chest. On the whole he was in splendid condition, for
a big man.

'Will you know me again?' he said drily and she saw
that he was watching her scrutinise him.

'Was I staring? I'm so tired I'm just not focusing,'
she said with disinterest. There was a flicker of something in his eyes. Vanity, perhaps. Dead beat he might
be, but he probably had the usual measure of male
pride in his muscles. 'Why would the red dots represent
you?' he said, drawing her attention back to the map
with its stickers.

'We stopped at all those towns marked with red, on
our tour. I wouldn't have marked them *red* myself, she
added drily. 'Pale pink, maybe.'

'Why's that?'

She shrugged. 'Heat, dust, flies. We acquired a
nuisance fan here——' She leaned over and pointed to
a town they'd visited two weeks ago. 'He followed us
from then on, with ever bigger bouquets of pink
carnations and proposals of marriage—nothing would
discourage him.'

'These proposals were to you?'

'Unfortunately.'

'How boring for you—being adored,' he said
sardonically.

She flushed, felt like saying it was more like being

hunted, even if the weapons were no more dangerous than a toothy grin and pink carnations. 'Awfully boring,' she drawled. 'And we broke some expensive equipment there——' She pointed to another town. 'I won't bore you with our box-office misfortunes—let's just say we didn't exactly set these places on fire. Definitely pale pink.'

His head came up and he looked hard at her. As if he would read her like a map too. Very cool, very detached was Boss Mackenzie. He probably only had ice-water connected in his shower.

He tossed her a folded towel. 'Be my guest, but make it short and sweet. We're low on fresh water in these parts.'

The water was deliciously warm. She washed away the grime of the day's heat and exertion, dressed in fresh clothes and freed her hair from its untidy braid. She emerged feeling human again, almost dreamy from the tranquilising effect of soap and water. Mackenzie had dressed in jeans and a shirt that he'd left unbut-toned. He was sprawled, apparently asleep in the swivel chair at his desk.

His eyes opened and Emma, brushing her hair over one shoulder, gave him a genuine smile. 'I'd thank you,' she said, 'except that in the circumstances it was the least you could do.'

Mackenzie blinked, stared. Their eyes held across the room, across the desk, for much longer than was conventional.

'Is that real?' he asked at last.

'What?'

'Your hair. The colour, I mean.'

Emma looked at him, conscious of the sudden change in atmosphere, a rise in her own personal tempo. 'Is yours?' she said, and he gave a snort of laughter at the idea of anything about himself not being genuine.

'Forget I asked. Tea or coffee?' His chair creaked as he got up and went to a counter behind the second desk, where steam shimmered over an electric kettle and mugs were set out in readiness.

'Tea, please.'

He took a teapot from a cupboard and spooned in tea then added boiling water. He held up a carton of milk and, when she nodded, poured from it into each mug. There was a short wait while he peered out of the window and absently swivelled the brown crock teapot to hasten the infusion. With the ease of practice, he held the lid in place with his index finger and poured with a certain delicacy. She couldn't say, though, that he looked any less formidable with a teapot rather than gauntlets and a knife.

'Well, this is more like it, Mackenzie,' she said, when he eventually handed her a mug of tea and offered biscuits from a jar. 'You're much more reasonable when you're tired. Or maybe it's because you don't have to act like the boss in front of your merry men.'

He sat down behind his desk and put his feet up, grandly complacent. 'I don't *act* the boss. I *am* the boss. And I'm always reasonable.'

'Men always think they're reasonable. But in a group they just can't help treating a woman as a joke.'

'Rubbish.'

'I wonder if you would have expected a man to just wait around for an hour for a few minutes of your time? Your crew wouldn't have leered and shouted insults to a man who had come with a genuine problem. If a man offered his hand, you would have shaken it.' His eyes flickered a bit at that, but he said nothing. 'Of course, if I could have arranged it, I would have got you alone.'

'And why's that?' he said softly.

'Well, isn't that obvious? Since I've seen you alone, you've invited me in to use your bathroom, provided

me with towels, tea and cookies,' she said cheerfully.
The silence had an irritable quality, as if he might be
regretting the generosity that allowed her to make this
comparison. Emma slid her hand around the back of
her neck, flipped her long hair forward over one
shoulder in a habitual gesture. The desk lamp picked
up a gleam in his half-closed eyes. Absently, she
combed her fingers through her hair but stopped self-
consciously when she saw that Mackenzie's attention
was riveted by the movement. She had a sudden urge
to go into the bathroom and braid her hair again, as if
she could braid up all this sudden tension with it.

'What a prince I am. Maybe I have an ulterior
motive now that I've got *you* alone—have you thought
of that?'

Just for a split-second, she faltered. She was no
weakling, but she would be no match for Mackenzie
with an ulterior motive. Adrenalin pounded unexpectedly into her system. Where Mackenzie was concerned, would she choose fight or flight?

'It was a joke. Relax. I've lit enough fires for one
day.'

Arrogant devil, deliberately playing on fears that he
never had to bother about. Men gave you every reason
to distrust them, then made you feel an idiot for doing
so.

'I wasn't bothered,' she said, stretching a point. 'I
can spot an ulterior motive a mile off. Men with ulterior
motives tend to overdo the charm.' She smiled to
reassure him that his level of charm raised him above
suspicion.

'Ouch,' he said, a glint of appreciation in his eyes.
'As a way of divining what's on a man's mind, it sounds
risky.'

'It's not just the phony charm that gives a man away,
believe me. Besides, I think I know what's uppermost
on your mind right now.'

'Oh, yes?' he challenged. By the light of the desk lamp, his eyes were mere slits with a reflected glitter. His swivel chair moved complacently from side to side.

'You're wondering if you should have camped at the fire-break, until morning. You're thinking about wind changes and sparks and the school so close and whether you should go back.' The swivelling stopped abruptly. 'You keep glancing at your watch, you see, and looking out of the window at the tree, to see if it's moving in the wind, I imagine.' She took a sip of her tea, quite enjoying his silence. Mackenzie raised his cup in a salute of a kind. 'Do you read tea-leaves too?'

She grinned. 'Only people.'

'Like books?'

'Some books are more puzzling than others. I can't decide, for instance, if you are simply pragmatic, loyal or kind.' She cast the whites of her eyes at the J. Clements painting so prominently displayed on his wall. He laughed but he said nothing to reveal whether it was kindness, loyalty, pragmatism or sheer lack of taste that had prompted him to hang it there.

'Are you going to sleep in that chair?' she asked, hoping that she might get to stretch out on his divan for an hour or so before she returned to the tortures of the van.

'If you have to ask, then you really can't read my mind.'

'Relieved, Mackenzie?'

'More than you might think.'

His eyes were open again and for a moment there was something glittering in them and Emma stared, reaching for it, her pulses quickening, but it was gone and she decided it was another illusion. After all, she'd got him confused with a dead kangaroo earlier. 'You can have the divan,' he said.

He turned off the lamp and the office was dark, save for the thin stripes of moonlight that filtered through the blinds on the door. His chair creaked a bit then he was silent. Emma didn't expect to sleep but she did, for over an hour. When she woke it was still dark and something was different. It took her a moment of adjustment to see that it was the movement outside the window. The tree was swaying in the wind. Emma got up and peered at Mackenzie. He was slumped sideways in his chair, one arm propping up his head, the other dangling over the side of the chair. Only exhaustion would allow him to sleep in such discomfort and she was reluctant to disturb him. For a few minutes she padded around, looking out of the window and when several stronger gusts rattled the tree, she turned on the desk lamp and bent to touch his shoulder. 'Mackenzie.'

He came up out of the chair, grasped her arms and stared groggily at her. Emma was feeling groggy herself, hauled unexpectedly against his bulk, his breath hot on her cheek.

'The wind's come up. I thought you might want to know.'

His eyes cleared and he put her aside and went to the window. He grunted, apparently in agreement with her assessment, then retrieved his belt from the smoky pile of discarded protective clothing. He looked at Emma, who had her head tilted as she quickly braided her hair. 'What do you think you're doing?'

'Thought I'd come along. Have you got a spare torch?'

He turned his back and put on the belt, clipped his torch to it. 'I'm not taking you.'

'Two could check for sparks quicker than one. I probably won't get to sleep again anyway. And I wouldn't mind seeing what it's like out in the bush at night.'

'You want the thrill of a nocturnal bush experience, go join a safari,' he said bluntly. 'Stay here, count sheep or seats, whatever a theatre director counts. The last thing I need out there is a screaming female.'

The door closed behind him. Hands on hips, Emma stared after him, heard a motor start and cut out, then nothing more. A few moments later there came another slam of a car door and footsteps. Keys jangled in the office door and Mackenzie strode in. Any civilised idea that he might have repented his rudeness and come to take her up on a perfectly reasonable offer to help vanished.

'My truck won't start,' he said tightly. 'I need a vehicle and it would save time if I borrowed yours. May I have the keys?'

He had his hands out, expecting the keys to be obediently slapped into it, and so powerful was his own expectation that she took up her bag and picked out the keys without question.

'Great,' he said, coming closer to take what he wanted.

Emma drew back, annoyed to find herself falling in with his demands after he had been so darned insulting. It reminded her of times she'd rather forget and of Simon, whose angelic good looks and beautiful manners were some excuse at least for her willingness to do his bidding. But Mackenzie! She held the keys to her breast.

'My van is at your disposal, Boss,' she said, and as he impatiently reached for the keys she added, 'This screaming female is driving.'

The van swayed and jolted over the same route she'd taken just a little more than twelve hours earlier. She felt Mackenzie's gaze shift sharply to her several times. Probably suffering withdrawal symptoms from not being in the driver's seat. 'I'm surprised you didn't just wrestle the keys from me, Mackenzie.'

'I'm beat but I'm not stupid,' he muttered, making it

sound as if he would be no match for her. Puzzled, she took her eyes from the road for a moment to look at him just as something ran in front of the van. Emma over-reacted, swerving wildly to miss the creature, and Mackenzie lurched over and grabbed the wheel with both hands, cursing.

She braked and the van stopped, shuddering gently by the side of the track. Emma passed a trembling hand over her face. Suddenly, her reserve energy ran out and she could scarcely stay upright. 'Sorry. I hit a kangaroo on the road yesterday—killed it. The first time I've ever killed anything. Such a beautiful creature. I didn't want to do it again——'

'For Pete's sake, Emma, that was a rabbit. Vermin, a pest. You could have turned the van over!'

'All right, all right! I'm sorry. I know *you* wouldn't lose any sleep over killing some poor thing on the road, but I'm not used to it.' In fact, she was trembling, as affected as she'd been when she hit the kangaroo.

Emma became aware that she was leaning against him, that his arm was hooked over her seatback and almost encircling her. She shifted a little away, not far enough to escape the warmth of his body. Mackenzie didn't move a muscle.

'I was half dreaming about it when you came along tonight—the kangaroo.' She turned her head to look at him. There was that glitter in his eyes again that made her throat dry.

'And me,' he said.

'What?'

'You must have dreamed of me, too.' His voice was low and grainy, rippling down the back of her neck almost as if he was touching her. '"I thought you were dead instead of the kangaroo," you said,' he went on, confident that he had put two and two together correctly. Emma stared at him, wondering if he could possibly know just what a weakness she had for a voice like his.

'That wasn't a *dream*, Mackenzie,' she said, rallying. 'That was a *fantasy*—running you down in the van.'

He chuckled, and the sound would have been pleasant except for the edge of complacency on it.

'You seem to be flattered by my violent reactions,' she said drily.

'I'd—prefer lukewarm reactions, all things considered.'

She frowned. 'What do you mean?'

He looked away, along the path of the headlights where moths fluttered. Smoke swirled into the illumination and vanished again into blackness. 'I'm—almost engaged to be married,' he said.

She blinked at this abrupt change of subject. 'Engaged?' So, Mackenzie was spoken for. Why should she find that disappointing? He was an overbearing type, an autocratic, self-important man's man raised in an outpost where men were men and women were supposed to know their place. He didn't even have the saving grace of sophistication and good looks that had made Simon such fun in the beginning. Just what she avoided like the plague. Even so, she felt vaguely depressed.

'Well, congratulations,' she said. 'But I don't see why you're suddenly telling me this in the middle of the night, in the middle of the road.'

'Don't you?'

Emma put a hand to her head, wondering if maybe she'd bumped it when the van swerved. 'Have I missed some vital piece of——' she began, when she grasped the significance of his tone, the meaningful look in his eyes. Lukewarm reactions, he'd prefer, because he was almost married, not violent reactions.

'You're passing through. I don't want any—complications,' he went on, expanding on his theme.

Emma's mouth dropped open. 'Are you declaring yourself *out of bounds*?' she said, astonished.

He gave a snort. 'You know what I'm saying.'

Blood rushed to her face. Now she suddenly remembered the stray references to her as a huntress, lying in wait, the hint that she enjoyed having Wayne Street worshipping her, the peculiar look he'd given her when she said she should have sought him out alone. 'You're unusual,' he'd told her and she'd known at the time it was anything but a compliment. He had her taped as the predatory type and himself as her target! His conceit took her breath away.

'I've been around a long time, Emma, and you're a grown woman. You know what was happening between us.'

'Perhaps you'd like to spell it out for me.'

'Physical attraction,' he said brutally. 'Chemistry. Something. Nothing I've ever. . . I'm damned if I know.'

There was resentment in these last words but bewilderment too and Emma's heart lurched at the admission from a man so sure of himself. It was a small triumph that the rock-like Mackenzie felt something for her but one that blossomed and died in the space of moments. It was nothing more than the physical attraction he'd quoted with such distaste. Her soul shrivelled at the thought.

He looked thoughtfully at her and, as if to console her for his harsh words, said, 'But if I *were* free. . .' His magnificent voice tapered off, inviting her to imagine the delights on offer—if only. 'But I'm not,' he said abruptly, bringing down the curtain on her imaginings before she went wild.

'You arrogant——!' Emma cast around for words. 'Listen, whether *you* were free or not doesn't matter, because you're not *my* type.' He listened with a singularly annoying expression. Emma hated herself for experiencing even a faint attraction to him. 'You're rude, sexist, self-centred, pompous, conceited—and greedy.'

'Greedy?' he protested.

And wasn't that revealing? The man didn't object to labels of sexism, rudeness and conceit—he probably thought they were compliments. 'You're telling me to keep my distance, but you wouldn't mind some admission from me that I'm interested in you. That way you get to stroke your ego twice, and I call *that*——' she stabbed an index finger at his shoulder '—greedy.'

'Don't do that,' he said, with the edges of his teeth together.

'And let's clear up this little matter of what might have been, if only *you* were free,' she said. 'You're insulting me with some Hollywood image of actresses—itinerant bits of fluff who think nothing of breezing into town, having an affair with the bossman for a week, then moving on. I'm not like that. I don't know anyone who is. Do you have such a low opinion of all women, or is it only me?'

'I can certainly plead innocent to thinking of you as a bit of fluff,' he said, rubbing the spot where she'd jabbed him.

'How dare you make a joke of this?' she hissed. 'How *dare* you?'

Her anger was intense but she wasn't sure that she'd been about to jab him again. At any rate, Mackenzie must have thought it possible, for he grabbed her wrist. Absolute quiet. Just the van motor, vibrating and her own blood pounding in her ears. Her breath and Mackenzie's. His chest rose and fell and she fancied she could see the fabric of his shirt expand and contract with the beat of his heart.

All her denials seemed suddenly pathetic. The tension between them might have been generated by anger but it was something else now, as if ordinary ingredients—the still dark bush outside, the smoke from smouldering earth and the body warmth of two strangers—were being blended in some weird alchemy to produce—what?

His fingers repositioned themselves on her wrist, his thumb shifted on the soft inner flesh. Emma felt the same sensation that she'd felt at his voice. Her captive fingertips touched his shoulder and she wanted to lay her hands along those rugged shoulders, and she wondered how it would be to kiss that implacable mouth. He raised her hand, pulled a fraction, moving her closer. Emma tried to remember if Simon had ever made her feel like this before it all went wrong, but Simon, whose image had been etched so sharp for so long, was just a fuzzy memory compared to Mackenzie's substantial presence. But just the thought of Simon was enough to remind her of other, more fathomable madnesses and she drew back.

He held her still, his thumb on her pulse and she could claim it was anger that made it so strong and fast. But if she didn't do something, Mackenzie would never believe that. With some urgency, Emma felt with her free hand for her lucky charm but it was in the wrong pocket. Damn.

'What's her name?' she said huskily.

Moments passed. 'Libby,' he said at last.

The name worked like a charm. All the silent, alchemic energy fizzled. Libby. Abracadabra.

He released her hand.

'Libby. Is that short for Elizabeth?' she asked, studiously polite. As if she cared.

'Elisa,' he answered, with a sardonic smile.

Emma was shaken. She hated herself for that brief moment of craving. A man she hardly knew. A man like Mackenzie! Thank heaven he was almost married. She felt she'd been hauled back from the edge of a vertical cliff. Thank you, Libby.

'So, when did you propose to your Libby?' she said, deliberately invoking the name again. 'Did you get down on your knees, Mackenzie?'

He smiled. 'There was no specific occasion—more a gradual realisation that we would be good together. . .'

'How romantic! On your twentieth wedding anniversary you can look back and say "Remember when we came to the gradual realisation that we'd be good together?"'

Mackenzie seemed lost in private thoughts. He peered up at the moon through the windscreen. 'I'm thirty-two. Time to settle down and start a family. I'd waited a long time for——'

For what? she wondered. For the nameless magic? For the right woman? Then he'd found both in Libby. She felt a curious sense of loss when she had nothing to lose, a momentary surge of jealousy for a woman she didn't know and a longing for something she didn't really believe existed. It had to be the moon and the smoke and insomnia.

'I think you're just in time. A family will make you more human, Mackenzie.'

He laughed softly then looked at her. 'What about you? Are you the marrying kind?'

Emma looked out the window. Trees stood black against an indigo sky, picked out by moon and starlight. The smell of smoke was strong in the air. Yes, she could have said. She had been the marrying kind, once. But she was not the *re*marrying kind.

'I like my work, I like my house, I like my name. I've never met a man who wouldn't demand I give up at least one if not all of them.'

'You wouldn't give up those things for a man?'

'Why should I?' she said hardily, thinking of Simon-take-all.

'Very bohemian.'

'There's an old-fashioned word. Nobody says "bohe-mian" any more.'

'I'm an old-fashioned man.'

Emma gave a shudder. 'I'm a new-fashioned woman. What about Libby?'

'Libby suits me down to the ground.'

Under his heel perhaps? 'Poor Libby.'

He laughed, secure in the knowledge that Libby was the most fortunate of women, and suggested that he drive, because there were another odd million or so rabbits in the vicinity and he didn't want to be sacrificed to save a pest. And Emma felt so in charity with him as a prospective family-man that she ignored his sar-casm and agreed.

The burn-site was desolate in the moonlight. The wind shook the living leaves high on the trees and rattled the burned ones lower down. Smoke drifted and wreathed through the tree-trunks. It took Mackenzie forty minutes to check out the area, tramp-ing over ground still warm from burning, a water spray unit on his back. Emma took a torch and walked the perimeter, defying Mackenzie's prediction that she would be screeching for help within minutes. It was an eerie experience all the same, and only stubbornness kept her from running when the van came into view again. The breeze had dropped by the time Mackenzie reappeared.

'Everything all right?' she asked.

He dumped the backpack and torch in the van and shed his gloves. 'There were a few sparks still burning. I doused them,' he said.

They didn't speak on the way back. The physical effort had driven their exhaustion so deep that nothing mattered except to lie down and sleep. All she remem-bered was an amicable silence. She didn't remember walking into the office or stretching out on the divan. She didn't remember taking of her shoes and loosening the catch on her bra. But when she woke in the morning she was barefoot and almost bare-breasted and in bed with a big, hairy man with a scratchy day-old beard and no trousers.

'What on earth——?' Emma shot upright, prompted by some subtle noise she didn't trouble to identify because of more pressing priorities. Her shirt had come adrift and was pinned down by Mackenzie's weight and, feverish to wrap it around her before he woke, she twisted and tugged but succeeded only in dragging the collar down, exposing her shoulder. Mackenzie stirred and propped himself up on an elbow, so close in the confines of the divan that his stubbled jaw scraped her bare skin. He rubbed the back of his neck and muttered, 'What the hell. . .? I don't remember——' He glanced at the swivel chair but his eyes came back to Emma and slid down to her exposed shoulder. It seemed to mesmerise him. She gave three sharp tugs on her shirt-tail and he obligingly raised himself to release it. Without looking at him, but supremely conscious of him, Emma pulled her shirt around her. When the collar caught on her hair, Mackenzie reached out and lifted her plait. She looked at him then and the sensory signals that she'd been trying to block out came through sharp and clear. He was close enough for her to see every bristle on his jaw, every pore in his rough-grained skin and the thin rim of red beneath his smoke-irritated eyes. Green eyes. Mackenzie didn't move a muscle, just leaned there, half naked, like some massive statue, his hand closed around her plaited hair so that she felt the slight drag on her scalp. The tips of his fingers touched her neck and her nervous system over-reacted wildly to the sensation, turning it into something languorous, exciting, dangerous. There was a charm that worked against this alchemy, but looking at Mackenzie's mouth she couldn't remember what it was.

The subtle noises escalated into a rattling and the door suddenly opened. The woman who came in stood there, open-mouthed, mutely jiggling the key from the lock. In one hand she held a basket in which various items of food could be seen. There was no attempt at discretion on her part, no averting of the eyes. On the contrary, she stared at Mackenzie then Emma with sly curiosity.

'Well, well, who's in bed with the Boss?'

Emma furiously buttoned her shirt. Cursing under his breath, Mackenzie got up, turned his back to the woman at the door and picked up his trousers. Emma was presented with a close view of hairy, muscular thighs and underpants patterned with tiny grey and black parasols. He scowled down when he saw her glazed expression, snatched his shoes from the floor and strode to the privacy of the bathroom, with, it seemed to Emma, cowardly speed.

Without looking back he made an introduction of sorts.

'Emma Spencer—meet J. Clements.'

CHAPTER THREE

THERE were nights when the chemistry was just right. In fifteen years of stage-work Emma could remember the times when the magic had happened. The same play might go on night after night, satisfactorily workmanlike, then out of nowhere would come that spark that lit up the players, electrified the workmanlike performances, crossed the footlights to touch the audience and suddenly the energy would zap back and forth. Chemistry.

Tonight wasn't one of those nights. The community hall was two-thirds full which was amazing, considering the economic bite of the drought and their unfortunate criticism of local heroes. The audience was slow to respond but the consensus back-stage was that they had been won over. Maybe most of them, Emma thought. But she'd seen Mackenzie in the audience and she knew he was anything but won over. He had been coldly furious when he'd emerged fully dressed from his office bathroom that morning. And Joyce Clements had fanned his fury with all the irreverence of someone who had known him from childhood. She was his mother's cousin and now his housekeeper and it might have been devotion that brought her into town with a 'proper' breakfast after he'd been away all night, but she seemed to find a malicious pleasure in catching him out. Emma felt a malicious pleasure herself, that Mackenzie had at least one female in his life who didn't quite know her place.

'I feel like Red Riding Hood, come to visit with a basket of goodies,' Joyce had said. 'The thing is, I can't decide who's the big, bad wolf.' She gave a curious gasping sound at this, which Emma divined was laughter. Joyce was perhaps sixty, so weathered by the outback sun that she seemed to be made entirely of brown hessian. Her amusement gathered around her eyes and mouth in stringy drapes.

'I feel you might have got the wrong idea,' Emma said stiffly, foreseeing further damaging stories circulating in town about the theatre floozie falling into bed with the boss man. 'I was sleeping in my van because of a mix-up with accommodation and Mackenzie very kindly——' she paused over the description, looking at Mackenzie's murderous expression as he made a phone call '——offered me somewhere to sleep.'

'"To save you from the foggy, foggy dew",' Joyce said with relish.

'Then we went out to check the burn-off site when the wind came up and we were so exhausted when we got back that we must have just——' Emma waved a hand at the divan, giving up on the explanation. Sometimes there was nothing so lame as the truth.

Joyce's sharp eyes grew sharper still. 'You went out to the site with Mackenzie—in the middle of the night? Doesn't sound like the Boss to let a woman tag along.'

'I didn't *tag* along. I drove him there.'

Mackenzie snorted. 'I'm lucky to be alive.'

Emma was tiring of his temper. 'Let's hope your luck holds out, Mackenzie,' she snapped.

A peculiar expression settled on Joyce. She looked Emma over carefully, her lips ruched. Emma had the feeling that she had just passed some test when the woman began unpacking the basket and said, 'You want some of Matt's breakfast? You must be hungry after all your—exertions last night.'

This last was said deadpan but Mackenzie heard, and said a few sharp words about housekeepers minding their own business and not jumping to conclusions before he went out. Joyce gave her gasping cackle at this and proceeded to set out cereal and make toast in a toaster she pulled from the basket. Faced with such generosity, Emma was even more embarrassed if it was possible. 'I think I should tell you before someone else does, that we—my crew—said some unflattering things about your paintings in the pub yesterday.'

Joyce poured some tea and said, 'Yeah, I heard. Damned cheek, I reckon. Now, tell me about yourself. Born and bred in Sydney?'

Rather relieved at this philosophical reaction, Emma found herself telling Joyce quite a lot more about herself than she intended. When Mackenzie returned, his hands covered in grease, Joyce packed up her things, unfazed by his rejection of the breakfast she'd brought to him. Emma packed up her things too, anxious to be gone before a secretary arrived to complicate matters. Mackenzie followed her outside, wiping his hands on a paper towel.

'Are you always this much trouble?' he said, as he retrieved his boots and torch from her van. His own truck had a stranded look, its bonnet propped open and several tools lying in defeat beside it.

'A rhetorical question, I take it,' she said stiffly.

'Until you turned up, all I had to worry about was the drought and bushfires.' He slammed the van door. 'Serves me right for feeling sorry for you. I invite you in to take a shower and look!' He made a gesture that took in his crippled truck and Joyce, who smirked as she drove away in an ancient Land Rover coated with dust.

Emma eyed him with dislike. 'Your car trouble is nothing to do with *me*, Mackenzie. And if our booking had been made as agreed, or you had made some serious effort to redress the mistake, I wouldn't have been around when Red Riding Hood arrived with your toast and marmalade.'

'I should have let you sleep in your van.'

'You should have kept your trousers on.'

'I don't remember taking them off,' he said, glaring at her across the van roof.

'Well, don't look at *me*.'

But he did look, comprehensively, and she felt sure he saw nothing he liked this morning, not even her hair which she had braided so tightly into a coil on top of her head that her eyebrows were permanently raised. 'I don't know why you're so angry anyway. If anyone has a right to be angry, it's *me*! A man can easily survive the scandal of being found in bed with a woman. Even if he *is* almost married. If the story gets out, women will disapprove but forgive you because, after all, it's in men's nature, isn't it? They'll blame *me* for tempting you! The men will think you're a real stud. As for me—well, there's no shortage of adjectives for a woman who is dicovered in bed with a man of short acquaintance——'

'Of short what?' he murmured, apparently appeased by the reminder of the double standard that operated in his favour.

'If you can iron out the accommodation arrangements by tonight, then we can probably stay out of each other's way until the celebrations are over,' she snapped.

'It's a small town,' he pointed out. 'I take it, as you are so concerned about your own reputation, that I can rely on your—discretion about last night?'

The implication being, Emma thought, that only self-interest would stop her from blabbing. 'I won't tell that the Boss wears parasol-printed undies and snores——'

'I don't snore,' he said catagorically.

'And talk in your sleep,' she added for good measure.

Mackenzie had pooh-poohed the idea, but edgily, as if the idea of giving away anything about himself was a threat to his existence. Which made it the more amazing that Mackenzie had all but admitted to a weakness for her the night before. He must have hated himself in the light of day. No wonder he didn't like her. On the stage, she felt his animosity now, beaming strongly to her from the third row.

Mackenzie had consulted his files and found no arrangements made for their accommodation. No apology was forthcoming, but Emma had to admit he had gone into action and persuaded Col to double up some of his regulars so that the Shoelace crew could have rooms at the pub for two nights. Where they would stay after that was anyone's guess. Emma supposed Mackenzie would let her know in his own good time, after the show tonight. As they took final bows, Emma glanced at Mackenzie, who sat with his arms folded across his chest as he had throughout the performance. She couldn't make out who was seated next to him.

After the show, a ladies' charity committee served tea and cakes while the audience met the cast. Emma turned around and there was Mackenzie, making inroads into a huge slice of caraway seed cake. He wore the conservative dress clothing of a country man—grey trousers, pale blue shirt, woven wool tie, serviceable shoes. A tweedy jacket was slung over his shoulder. Nothing trendy or fashionable about Mackenzie. A rock, immune to the rush tides of fashion. He would probably look like this in thirty years' time. It should have been a more depressing thought. When he met her eyes it was with the air of one who had known for some time exactly where she was and that she was looking his way. Emma looked around, wondering whether Libby was the good-looking, thirtyish woman in tan linen helping out with the ladies' committee.

She collected a cup of tea and went over to him. His face was clean-shaven, his hair tamed and smooth for the first time since she'd met him. In some decent clothes he could look quite striking, Emma decided. 'I thought it might be you,' she said. 'But I was afraid you might make another cowardly exit after the show, before I could find out where we'll be staying after we leave Col's hotel.'

Tonight she was wearing heels and very nearly matched him for height. She had changed into trousers and a matching emerald silk shirt, the tailored clothes she favoured to minimise the sometimes embarrassing fullness of her breasts and hips. In scooped necklines and full skirts and floaty fabrics she tended to look like a sixties sex goddess, and Emma avoided the image like the plague. Mackenzie flicked a glance over her that made her wonder for a moment if she'd slipped up tonight. He finished his slice of cake at leisure and took a mouthful of tea, loftily choosing to ignore her reminder that he'd left her making bedside explanations to Joyce this morning. 'Thought it might be me?'

'In the audience. I could tell I was coming up against a stone wall with someone. And when I thought of stone walls——'

'You thought of me. I'd no idea being onstage was such a psychic experience,' he said drily.

'Actually, I *saw* you in the audience,' she admitted. 'But sometimes it can be almost psychic. You can actually feel a centre of resistance in the audience, or the opposite, of course.'

'What is the opposite?'

'Communication, I suppose,' she said slowly. 'Hard to describe. A sort of short-circuiting of all the usual means of communication—straight from here——' she spread a hand to her chest '—to—someone out there.' Under his cool, prosiac gaze the gesture and the subject seemed suddenly corny. 'Chemistry,' she said, then wished she hadn't. They had already discussed chemistry. Her face reddened but no one would notice because the off-stage lighting in the community hall was as excruciatingly bad as everything else about it.

'About your accommodation,' Mackenzie said, gazing down into his empty mug as if he might read something from the tea-leaves.

'It's not tents, is it?' she said suspiciously.

'All your requirements will be met.'

'What's this place called?'

He gave a quirky smile. 'It's *called* Falkner's Place. You'll be accommodated in the homestead—four bedrooms and breakfast, share bathrooms.'

Emma frowned. 'Homestead? Out of town, then. Where could we rehearse?'

'There are several outbuildings. The hangar——'

She cast her eyes up. 'Well, I suppose rehearshing in a hangar is no worse than anything else on this tour. If our luck runs true to form, we'll probably break the drought for you.'

Mackenzie looked at her enquiringly.

'It would be priceless if the first rain in years happened during the finale performance in the amphitheatre,' she said, absently taking her gold lighter from her pocket to turn it over and over in her hand.

Frowning, he watched the motion. 'Rain could only enhance our celebrations.'

Emma smiled. 'I suppose so. But while all you Catastrophians might delight in sitting out in drought-breaking rain, I can tell you that my crew wouldn't fancy performing in it. It might sound silly, but do you have any wet-weather contingency plans?'

He looked quizzical. 'It won't rain. But if it did, no one would get wet. The whole place is under roof.'

'Under *roof*? An amphitheatre? But I understood it was a natural formation—seats carved out of rock, Roy Jackson said on the phone. He sent me a diagram——' Emma looked hard at Mackenzie. 'Is there something I should know about this place?'

He weighed her up, considering how she might react, and Emma had a premonition of more trouble.

'The Amphitheatre is actually a local name for the place, rather than a geographical description.' He paused. 'It's a cave. On my land, in fact.'

Emma gaped. She looked left, then right, lest any of her crew overhear, then moved confidentially close to Mackenzie.

'A *cave*? A cave called the Amphitheatre? Why wasn't this spelled out in the contract?'

'You should have checked if it wasn't clear.'

'Why should I check?' she hissed. 'It seemed crystal-clear to me. Where I come from, people call a cave a cave.' She grasped his arm. 'Promise me you'll say nothing to my people about this. I'll have to take a look at it first then pick the right time to tell them and I can't guarantee that they won't pack up and leave. They'd be entitled.'

'A temperamental lot, your people.'

'And if they were *your* people, your fabulous leader-ship would make them stay through pestilence and wildfire—you already told me,' she snapped, stung again by his attitude and her own feelings of failure.

Mackenzie looked pointedly at her hand, clenched on his arm, and she was conscious suddenly of the hard muscularity beneath the cotton sleeve. Of course he wouldn't want to be seen with a woman squeezing his arm, especially one he'd spent the night with, however innocently.

Just then he looked over and smiled at someone, a special kind of smile that made Emma turn to see who had softened those green eyes. A young woman detached herself from a greying middle-aged man and came towards them, her glossy brown bob flipping againt a rose-petal skin that marked her as very young indeed, out here where the sun quick-dried youth into middle-age. She was expensively dressed in a short

skirt, cropped jacket and some very good gold jewel-
lery. Her long, slim legs drew some attention. As she
came up to Mackenzie, he put his hand to her waist,
she leaned in close, brushing her cheek once, very
quickly against his broad shoulder. This town, Emma
thought dourly, was full of non-verbal communicators.
'Matt, are we leaving soon?' she asked. 'Dad has an
early start with the horses tomorrow and I'm flying to
Broken Hill to do some shopping.'

'Soon, kitten. Tell John I have some minor business
things to attend to first.' Mackenzie smiled fondly down
at her. He transferred his gaze after a moment to
Emma, reminding her silently of her promise of discretion. He looked, she thought, slightly embarrassed,
but it was hard to be sure with Mackenzie. 'Libby,
meet Emma Spencer, director of the Shoelace Theatre
Company.'

Libby looked Emma over with the detachment she
probably showed for her Dad's horses. 'Oh, yes, you
had a small part in the play, didn't you? You looked
much younger on stage. Does director mean you direct
plays or what?'

'Occasionally. But I own the theatre—or rather, me
and the bank and the investors,' Emma said, rather
taken aback by this frank and dewy young thing. How
old was she—twenty, twenty-one? And Mackenzie was
thirty-two. *Kitten*. She met his gaze and looked away.
It was no business of hers if Mackenzie was cradle-
snatching. 'I worked in theatre on and off since I was
twelve and, when my grandmother left me some
money, I talked some other people into investing with
me in an old shoe factory.'

'But—I mean, you must have someone to run it for
you?' Libby said ingenuously.

'I run it myself, along with some very good staff. A
close friend of mine is standing in for me at present to
handle a special project.'

'Is he an actor or something?'

'She could be described as an actor or something,' Emma said drily, not sure why she found Libby so abrasive. 'Ami's a dancer and actor, but her field is really special effects and make-up.'

'You're both jacks of all trades, then,' Libby said, making them sound flighty and inconsequential.

'Actors learn to be just that. The unemployment rate in the business is usually over ninety-five per cent,' Emma said. 'So, tell me, what is it your father does with horses?'

The girl made a gesture that said everyone in these parts knew what people did with horses. 'Oh, my father breeds racehorses as a kind of hobby,' she said briefly as if any more detail might overload a city mind. 'If you like, you can come and have a look around while you're staying at Matt's place. Our land runs alongside his.'

So he was marrying the girl next door. 'Oh, we'll be staying at Falkner's Place, not Mackenzie's. Is that far from you?'

Libby gave a peal of laughter and squeezed Mackenzie's arm. 'Falkner's Place *is* Matt's place, didn't you know?'

'What?' Emma's gaze went to Mackenzie.

'Everybody around here just knows,' Libby said. She turned away to tell another local how Emma had amusingly thought Falkner's Place belonged to people called Falkner. There was nothing like local jokes to get an audience laughing, Emma thought darkly. They would laugh even louder at the illogicality of city people who thought an amphitheatre had no roof! And the amphitheatre-cave was on Mackenzie's land. She chewed at her lower lip. So there had never been any chance that they could stay out of each other's way, whatever happened. Why hadn't he told her that? Libby walked away and the last trace of Mackenzie's

geniality went with her. He looked at Emma, a frown
cutting a double line between his brows, his green eyes
hard again, his mouth thinned in irritation. Mine host,
she thought, her heart sinking.

'You can't dislike the idea any more than I do,' she
said. 'I suppose it was a last resort?'

'What do you think?' he said.

Emma grimaced. Of course he would have exhausted
all other options before having them at his place. 'In
that case, we thank you for your hospitality,
Mackenzie. One problem though—I have to be in town
several days to drill the schoolkids and the community
groups for the opening. I can't afford to waste over two
hours every day travelling back and forth.'

'I have to be in town myself,' he said shortly. 'We'll
fly in.'

'Fly?' she repeated. 'Oh.'

'You might remind your crew of the fire danger, to
take care with cigarette butts and——' he glanced down
at the lighter that Emma turned convulsively end on
end in her hand '—and naked flame. Our fresh water
supply is adequate but there are rules for the use of
water in drought times and I expect guests to co-
operate. Also, there are some areas of my land that
are off limits, so you'll need permission to go sightsee-
ing. Is that clear?'

Emma's eyes sparkled. 'I think you've explained
exactly what is out of bounds. As I said last night, it
really isn't necessary.'

He hesitated then and for a crazy moment she
thought he might shake hands to seal this understanding between host and guest. But he merely inclined his
head and moved away to Libby and her father, leaving
Emma forewarned but not forearmed.

Fire, water and Mackenzie. To be avoided or taken
in very small doses.

CHAPTER FOUR

FROM the air, the early buildings of Falkner's Place homestead took on a very different character from the later additions. They were compact, crouched under the protection of high, steep roofs, defensive in the wide open spaces. The shadows of the helicopter rippled over the multi-faceted roofs and chimneys.

'They look like a cluster of survivors huddled together in the wilderness,' Emma said. 'I suppose the early settlers were accustomed to pretty English countryside. This must have looked stark and terrifying.'

She glanced at Mackenzie at the controls. He wore wrap-around reflector sunglasses and all she could see in them when he turned to her was a distorted version of her own face.

'Probably,' he said.

The homestead's sprawling, confident buildings added by generations more at home in the Australian landscape, were connected to the old by a network of covered, trellised walkways. A similar network of dusty tracks connected stables, a hangar, outbuildings and bores with windmills and a couple of small houses for station hands, each with their own fenced garden. A winding stretch of trees and grass marked the course of a creek which petered out into billabongs and water-holes, a dotted green line on the brown expanse. Birds flew up in alarm at the sound of the chopper.

Emma hadn't been prepared for the size of the place, the sheer complexity of the operation that Mackenzie ran. It was impossible not to be impressed with the range of his expertise—horseman, cattleman, businessman, pilot. Farming, as she'd realised when she'd seen the journals on insemination breeding methods and stock-feed research that filled Mackenzie's house, was a high-tech business. She turned in her seat to look back at the homestead where the tops of the olive trees flickered silver in the chopper's wake. Emma squinted as the sun flashed on the roof of the hangar. 'FALKNER' was painted in giant letters on the iron.

'Was there ever an owner called Falkner?' Emma asked, into the mouthpiece fitted to the earphones she wore. Mackenzie's blank sunglasses turned towards her. He wore overworked moleskins and a faded grey shirt bearing traces of its original blue in the overtaxed sleeve seams and around the pocket-stitching. Mackenzie looked set to wield a sledgehammer or rope a steer rather than work in his councillor's office in town, but Emma didn't ask him what his plans were. He was taking her into town and she was sticking to safe, impersonal subjects, and the origins of Falkner's Place seemed as safe as any.

'The Falkners are the pioneers of the district. Built here in 1840. Next week, I'll be opening the original house and the stables to the public,' he told her. 'Gertrude Falkner was the last of the family. Her brothers were killed in the war and she never married, ran the place herself until she was over eighty. Willed it to her cousin's son on the understanding that the name would be kept. He put in a manager and took down the sign out front, replaced it with an executive brass affair. His name was Winston so he changed the name to Winston Meadows.'

Emma looked down at the uncompromising expanses of dry, brown land. '*Meadows*?'

Mackenzie smiled but conceded, 'The place was greener then. He and his wife used to fly in from Sydney with their friends for house-parties until the novelty wore off and wool prices fell through the floor.

He let it run down, then sold off bits of the farm to keep it going. It used to be the biggest place around here but now it's one of the smaller. I bought it from him.'

And did what the insensitive heir had not—put up Gertrude's sign at the front gate again, painted the Falkner name on his new hangar. Emma studied him with renewed interest. She'd never met a man who wouldn't rather have his own name up in lights.

Save for fences, and occasional marches of power lines, all traces of inhabitation vanished. Barren outcrops of rock and bullock-bush. Patchy shade of redgum trees over bleached grass. The land rolled away in singed, brown folds and pleats to distant slate-blue hills. Somewhere out here had to be herds of the cattle and sheep that sustained the region but Emma saw only a few dozen scattered animals.

Mackenzie detoured to check out a show of smoke and discovered the only human activity between his place and Catastrophe, a farmer burning off some low scrub as a firebreak around a house. 'What mainly starts bushfires?' Emma asked. Another safe topic. She congratulated herself.

'Farmers burning a fire-break like that one, or burning out cured grass to get some green shoots for stock.' He glanced at her, as if gauging the depth of her interest before continuing. 'Railways. Tractors and machinery giving off sparks——'

'How do railways cause fires?'

'Power lines overhead. No shade because the trees and growth are cut back either side. It makes a long corridor through the countryside. The steel rails and the rock filler raise the air temperature over it, lower the humidity—that means the surrounding growth is drier than normal. Wind moves faster because of the tunnelling effect and the air turbulence of the trains fans any sparks. Ideal conditions for fire, if you add carriages full of smokers, some of them careless enough to toss a stub out the window. Five per cent of fires in this country are started by careless smokers.' He glanced at her, his expression unreadable because of the glasses. 'You'll have to be careful.'

'I don't smoke. I gave it up years ago.'

'You carry a lighter.'

'That's my lucky charm.' She took out the lighter and flipped it nonchalantly. 'Are many bushfires started on purpose—for kicks, I mean.'

The helicopter shuddered. Mackenzie cursed. 'Arsonists account for about seven per cent,' he said.

'Why do they do it? Is it the feeling of power, or the sight of the fire itself?'

He glanced at her again and she had the feeling suddenly that the subject was not so safe as she thought, but wasn't sure why. 'Both, probably. But they say a lot of firebugs hang around to watch what they've started so maybe the sight of it is important to them.'

In one of those irrelevant leaps of the mind, she remembered Steve saying, 'She's beautiful, isn't she?' about the fire.

'Why did you ask that?' Mackenzie said.

'Why not? You seem to have all the statistics.'

'Am I boring you?'

She gave him a non-committal smile. 'What about lightning and freak things like that?'

'I heard of a bushfire caused by an eagle once,' he said. 'Its wings shorted across some high tension lines and it burst into flames and fell on to dry grass. Set the place alight.'

Emma grimaced. 'What a horrible thing.'

'Yes. The fire took two days to put out.'

'Well, yes, that's awful too. But I meant—the eagle burning to death.'

The blank sunglasses turned toward her again. He

grinned and the effect of it was like turning on a light in a dark room. What on earth, she thought, had led her to think Mackenzie had no looks? The man had all the unexpected attraction of the land below. A tough, no-frills, surviving kind of attraction that grabbed you on a level never experienced with the conventional beauty of plenty. Emma stole another look at him, uneasy with the idea. She didn't want to be reached by Mackenzie on any level.

The helicopter landed on a pad beside the showgrounds which consisted of a large grassed oval and a grandstand. The grounds were busy with horses and carts, oxen harnessed to drays, a few descendants of German and Chinese settlers bright in ethnic dress and schoolchildren holding coloured pom-poms.

Hands on hips, Mackenzie observed the confusion and said sardonically to Emma, 'You think you can sort this out into some kind of order for the opening—in four days?'

'That's what you've paid me for,' she said brightly.

'Isn't this an odd job for a theatre director and actress?'

'Times are tough, Mackenzie. A theatre director has to diversify. I designed one of these mass displays for a friend of mine—a schoolteacher—and started getting requests to take on more as paying propositions. I like it, it pays and it is a kind of theatre, though the purists would disagree.' She pointed out a phalanx of school-children. 'All those pom-poms will form a sort of flickering pattern as the kids stand and sit—worked roughly on the same principle as the Mexican Wave.'

Mackenzie looked sceptical. 'If you say so. I'll be back to get you this afternoon. Four-thirty.'

He walked away and, an hour later as she conferred with the various group co-ordinators, heard the heli-copter's clatter as he took off. I'll be back to get you. Emma felt a treacherous little ripple down her spine.

As an antidote, she prepared several other safe subjects
to occupy their flying time.

It set the tone for the following day. They were
polite and distant to each other, they talked about
beef-breeding technology and theatre management.
While Emma was away during the day, her crew
rehearsed the Shakespearian excerpts they would perform for the finale, to commemorate the performance
a hundred years ago, of the company of English and
American actors who had roamed across the west.
Fresh from New York, the intrepid Richard Niblett's
Travelling Troupe had performed in the Amphitheatre
when a flash flood had destroyed the new town hall,
and brought western culture to homesick settlers.
Emma could only hope that her players would prove as
intrepid as the ones they were supposed to emulate.
Emma kept her fingers crossed that they didn't find out
just how intrepid they were required to be before she
told them.

On this second evening at Falkner's Place, they had
sat at Mackenzie's baronial dining table and eaten
another of Joyce's unimaginative meals. Emma thought
if the boiled beef and potatoes was retribution for
criticising her paintings then it was overkill. Driven to
it, Bernie supplied several bottles from his private store
of red wine and endeavoured to give a recalcitrant
Joyce some diplomatic tips on cooking until Emma's
kicks under the table finally made contact with his
shins. So tired was she, from the exhausting day in the
hot sun, from avoiding Mackenzie and damping down
open warfare between Bernie and Joyce, that Emma
expected to sleep like a log. But once in bed she was a
bleary-eyed victim of insomnia again. At one in the
morning she finally got up, pulled on some jeans and a
shirt. She took her torch and went outside.

The quality of silence was matched by the splendour
of the night sky. The dogs raced to her, barking a

couple of times but flopped down again to sleep when they had re-established her credentials. The air was warm and soft and the starlight so bright that she had no need to switch on her torch. She strolled as far as the old stable building. Of brick, it was modelled on Georgian English farmbuildings and meant to nestle in under oaks and elms in green pastures. Here, its pretty proportions starkly outlined beside a lanky red-gum, it looked an awkward newcomer. The smell of horses and hay and tackle rose in her nostrils as she ventured into the building. She heard a soft whicker and shuffle as a horse moved. Her nerves jumped and she grimaced into the dark interior, wondering what on earth she was doing here in the middle of the night, with several very large, unpredictable beasts. She took out her torch to look at the pointwork on the windows, but fumbled and dropped it.

'Oh, damn,' she said under her breath and knelt to gingerly pat the straw-strewn floor. She remembered her lighter, flicked on the flame and held it at arm's length, bending to catch a glimpse of the torch. Something rustled behind her and she let out a squeak, thinking one of the horses had got out. But it was another large, unpredicable beast that leaned there against a post and shone a torch at her.

'Insomnia, Emma?'

'Mackenzie!' she gasped, pressing a hand to her breast. 'You frightened me. My heart's galloping.'

'Always so appropriate,' he said drily, flicking his torch around the stable.

Emma's body was on red alert, pumped up with adrenalin. Fight or flight? Which was the best option when confronted with Mackenzie on a dark, silent night? His torch-light shifted up over her extended hand, and the lighter with its wavering flame. 'I dropped my torch,' she said by way of explanation and turned back to where she felt it should be. But she couldn't find it, though she dragged her hand through hay and goodness knew what else. 'It must have rolled,' she said. 'I'll find it tomorrow.'

Mackenzie took the lighter from her and looked thoughtfully at it. When he noticed the inscription, he shone his torch closely at it.

'Hey, do you mind?' Emma said, trying to snatch it back. Mackenzie simply hunched away from her and she came up against biceps and a brawny shoulder and an elbow carved out of granite.

He read out loud. '"To Emma, who lights up my life. Simon."'

His look was contemplative. 'And did Simon light up Emma's life?'

Emma decided against another swipe at her property, defended as it was by so much muscle. 'He did for a while.'

Mackenzie tossed the lighter in his hand, weighing it. 'You must have had some candlepower. This is a very expensive present.'

She smiled wryly. 'Impressive, isn't it? Simon's presents always were.'

'You sound hard to please. What's wrong with it?'

'I'd already given up smoking for a month when he gave it to me.'

Mackenzie grinned. 'Not an observant man?'

'A busy man. Ambitious,' she said shortly. 'Preoccupied.' Except when Simon thought she could help him get what he wanted. Then he was very attentive, very persuasive. First the fabulous dinner, champagne, the mood music. Then, the next morning in the afterglow, 'I need your signature, darling. . .just a formality. . . don't worry about anything. I love you, I wouldn't do anything that wasn't good for you. . .'

'And did you forgive him, for being so unobservant?'

'Of course. He'd just given me a present—very expensive as you noticed. It would have been churlish of me to say that he should have noticed if the one who lit up his life was no longer lighting up anything else.'

He laughed softly. 'It's the thought that counts.'

'I think that was dreamed up by someone who couldn't be bothered making an effort.'

Mackenzie flicked the lighter on again, off again. His eyes were in deep shadow but glittered every time the flame came on. Emma looked at the outline of his hand, the warm flesh tones of his chest showing between his unbuttoned shirt. His hair was sticking out crazily, as if he'd just got out of bed. He slept, she knew, in a huge bed with an off-white Marcella coverlet. Joyce had casually showed the Boss's bedroom to her. 'He won't wear pyjama tops to bed, not even in winter,' she'd confided. 'Still, you already know he doesn't like wearing much in bed, eh?' The sly reminder had brought back memories of waking practically in Mackenzie's arms. Emma often wondered what would have happened if Joyce had not come in at that precise moment. She wondered again, now. The flame went on again. Off again. 'So, how come you call this your lucky charm?'

'It reminds me not to be a fool again. Can I have it back, please?' she said, wanting urgently to be reminded not to be a fool again. The man was almost engaged to be married to Libby. Libby, she said to herself several times, alarmed to find that the name was losing its power.

'Sure.' But as he came over to her, dropped it. She joined him and they searched on hands and knees for several minutes. 'We'll find your lucky charm tomorrow,' Mackenzie said at last, standing and hoisting her up with him. It was a move that brought her too close. She put out a hand to help retain her balance and it landed on his chest. 'And your torch,' he added, watching her intently. 'What?' she said distractedly, looking into his eyes. 'Oh, yes—my torch,' she said, having a struggle to remember it.

She found her torch herself the next morning, but failed to turn up her lucky lighter. It made her uneasy, edgy. In spite of the lousy luck they'd already had, in spite of the fact that she didn't consider herself superstitious, she felt the need of the lighter's smooth shape in her pocket.

Steve was taking off down one of the tracks on his motorbike when she came out of the stables. He detoured to her, kicking up a trail of dust.

'Hi, Emma.' He looked admiringly at her jungle green shorts, sleeveless safari shirt and her long, lightly tanned legs. She had plaited a khaki scarf into the loose braid she wore at the base of her neck. Mackenzie had passed through while she ate breakfast in Joyce's massive kitchen, and barely managed a nod in greeting. Steve's admiration and welcoming smile made a pleasant change. 'Hop on—I'll take you for a guided tour.'

'But don't you have work to do?' she asked.

Steve's smile was sunny. 'Nothing that won't wait.'

Emma hesitated. 'I have to meet your brother in about an hour and a half to go to the—the Amphitheatre,' she said. 'Ten-thirty, at the hangar,' Mackenzie had told her last night, if she wanted to see the cave before someone spilt the beans to her crew. Emma wasn't especially looking forward to being stuck alone with Mackenzie again. She was running out of safe subjects.

'I'll have you back in tons of time. Hop on,' Steve said, flashing his teeth. She hopped on. He revved the bike, dust spurted and Emma's anxieties were temporarily blown away in the slipstream. The sun shone, the sky was a stunning blue dome and she was with a handsome young man full of life and devilment. No complications, no unsafe subjects. She felt suddenly free and young and a bit crazy. The wind tugged at her hair and the wide open spaces sped by.

They stopped and watched cattle being herded through the yards to be drenched for ticks. Steve introduced her to a stockhand's wife who was hand-watering some impoverished-looking lettuce seedlings in the fenced garden around her cottage while two small black children shouted as they rode around on tricycles with bright red wheels. There was no sign of Mackenzie, only the gently undulating land and the creek drying up but still growing water-lilies here and there in billabongs and old slab-built byres and out-buildings and hides drying on a fence. Steve talked almost non-stop, pointing out features to her with a studied nonchalance that didn't quite hide his pride. Dust blew and her hair and the scarf came loose from the plait and her shorts rolled up with the jolting motion of the bike as Steve headed back to the homestead. It wasn't until the hangar came into view that Emma looked at her watch and realised she was ten minutes late.

In the hangar, Bernie and the others were rehearsing on a rectangle marked out with chalk. There was a tractor and what looked like a cultivator along one side of the hangar. The helicopter was outside alongside Mackenzie's battered utility truck. The vehicle was the dusty, indeterminate colour she'd noticed at his office, but now Emma saw that there were patches of the original clay-red colour where the sun hadn't faded the duco. The bonnet was up and Mackenzie appeared from behind it, wiping his hands on a cleaning rag.

Steve performed a showy little half-circle, to bring the bike to a stop by the truck. A muscle clenched in Mackenzie's jaw as he looked at Emma, her hair tousled and windblown, legs exposed by the disappearing shorts, her arms wrapped around Steve's waist. He grasped the edge of the truck's bonnet, slammed it shut with a resounding clang.

'I've been waiting fifteen minutes,' he said to Emma and without waiting for a response, said to his brother, 'You're supposed to be working.'

Steve shrugged. 'Just being hospitable to our guest.'

'Miss Spencer isn't wearing a crash helmet. Your "hospitality" could turn sour if you had a prang and she got hurt. She'd probably sue us.'

Emma opened her mouth to deny it, but Mackenzie went on, 'Besides, we are not running a guest house, we're running a farm.'

'*We're* not running anything,' Steve said sulkily. '*You* are.'

Emma got off the bike. 'Look, Mackenzie, I hope I haven't caused any trouble.'

Mackenzie gave her a look that said she hoped in vain. To his brother he said, 'No more joyrides, Steve. Get on with it.'

Red-faced, Steve smiled sheepishly at Emma and retrieved his manhood with some ear-splitting revs and a racing start. Dust billowed and through it, Emma saw Mackenzie throw open the passenger door of the ute. 'Let's go,' he said. As she got in, he plucked a beat-up hat from a shelf in the hangar, and skimmed it onto her lap. 'Wear this when we get out. You'll get sunstroke otherwise.'

Mackenzie put his foot down and the truck tore along one of the tracks that had recently been graded, to improve the track for the finale traffic, she supposed. It was just one more chore that Mackenzie had to attend to, like driving her out here today. She felt guilty that she'd kept him waiting. If he hadn't been so darned rude, she would apologise.

The truck stopped in the middle of nowhere. Mackenzie took out the large, metal cased torch he'd had with him last night and got out and slammed the door. As this seemed to be their point of departure, Emma got out too.

Dry grass as far as the eye could see. Plains and hollows and hills covered with it. Lonesome trees and crouching outcrops of rock. The sky was immense, the colour of heartbreak, pure blue. The sun burned down on her head. The cry of a crow came from a long way away and Emma saw the bird, just a speck circling over the emptiness. The crushing sense of her own smallness took her by surprise. She felt no bigger than the bird in this vast emptiness. It made her feel both attracted yet alienated. As if she was in the right place at the wrong time. Or was it the wrong place and the right time?

Emma sighed and dropped the Akubra on her head. 'So where's this cave?' she asked.

He slapped the torch a couple of times into the palm of his hand before he turned to her.

'Leave my brother alone.'

She gave a little cough of surprise. 'What?'

'He's already irresponsible enough. He doesn't need any encouragement.'

'*I* didn't inveigle Steve into showing me around,' she protested. 'He offered.'

'If he offers again, refuse him,' he said flatly.

Emma bristled. 'I see. So Steve's out of bounds too! Does he know that you go around stage-managing his private life?'

'I'm looking out for him. He's had enough trouble and I don't want him messed up by someone like you.'

'Someone like *me*?' She said the words carefully, as if they made up a foreign phrase. 'Just exactly what is a women like me?'

'You're mature, experienced, sophisticated. Steve's a boy and you're too old for him.'

'Is your child-bride aware of your prejudice against age differences?' she enquired with acid sweetness.

Small patches of white appeared each side of the mouth. Head thrust forward, shoulders hunched and hands on his hips, he looked fit to kill. She glanced nervously at the metal-cased torch almost crushed in one of those big hands. The classic blunt instrument, she thought wildly, and no witnesses. The only movement came from the crows that flapped around a redgum as if they were waiting for something. Bones to pick. Involuntarily, she took a step back from him.

'I'm looking out for him,' he said again, harshly. 'God knows it's hard enough because he goes walkabout for days on end and never tells me where. . . I just don't need you messing him up, OK? You're too——' He stopped, looked her over but couldn't seem to come up with a description. 'And he's susceptible, so I'm warning you now, just don't play games with him.'

'Games! For heaven's sake——'

'You've already got one poor fool adoring you, following you around with flowers. Can't you make do with him?'

Emma flushed deeply. The man made her out to be some cheap siren, luring men. 'Maybe you should mind your own business, Mackenzie. Steve's not a child and while I'm prepared to live by your rules as a guest, I think it's a bit much, interfering with my friendship with your brother.'

'Friendship!' he said with scorn. 'Honey, you came back with him this morning looking as if you'd been romping together in the hayfield.'

Emma's eyes blazed. 'I only romp in hayfields with *very* good friends!'

'Maybe you make friends very fast,' he said. 'You were coming on strong to me from the moment we met—"You've got green eyes",' he mimicked softly.

'You think that's coming on strong?' she said incredulously. 'Mackenzie, you've been in the backwoods too long.'

'All that stuff about reading my mind and feeling my vibrations in the audience—grabbing my arm——'

She was so hot now, it was unbearable. 'You're taking me out of context and you know it, as for grabbing you——'

'Honey, if I hadn't produced a fiancée backstage, I probably would have got an invitation to your hotel room, and *I* didn't even have to bring pink carnations!'

It hit her like a blow to the solar plexus and she hit back. Her hand connected solidly with his jaw in a slap that was startling in the sun-soaked silence. Mackenzie's head snapped to one side and his hat fell off. Emma watched the mark of her hand slowly redden on his skin, horrified by her own violence. Eyes locked on hers, Mackenzie rubbed two fingers over his jaw. It was oddly intimate, as if she'd put her mark on him in some other kind of passion than anger. Emma licked her lips and his eyes followed the movement.

'I—don't think I've ever done that before,' she said inanely, to break the silence. 'Not even to a theatre critic.'

To her relief, he gave a wry huff of laughter. He hefted the torch from hand to hand and transferred his attention to the horizon as if he might find some explanation there. His gaze swung back to a point in the distance and he reached through the open window of the truck to take out binoculars.

He raised them while Emma shaded her eyes and looked for a dust trail or a movement somewhere to account for this sudden shift in attention. Being belted by a woman was something he certainly took in his stride

'Cloud,' Mackenzie said, and after a moment, handed her the glasses.

'Oh—a rain cloud, do you think?'

Mackenzie shrugged as if reluctant to commit himself to such hopefulness. But she saw the glitter in his eyes

and a faint flush along his cheekbones to match the
fading mark of her hand. She peered through the
glasses, seeing nothing but blue. 'I can't see
anything——'

Mackenzie turned her shoulders a fraction. She felt
the contact of his hands, warm and heavy and stood
very still. Every detail of his hands was conveyed to
her through her skin sensors—the broad palms curved
over her shoulders, the angle of his thumbs pointing in
to her neck, the calloused fingertips lightly pressed into
the bare skin of her arms. The sun beat down and she
thought if they didn't move soon they might be baked
like clay here on the rocks and the red-brown earth
that had been baking in the sun for centuries. Two
statues in the right place and the wrong time. It all
seemed of a piece—the feel of his hands on her and the
heat rising from the earth and the expectant hush of
the empty land all around.

Then his hands slid from her and she breathed again
and tilted the glasses shakily and saw the cloud. It was
tiny, hardly drought-breaking. 'Perhaps there are more
following it,' she said, handing back the binoculars.
Maybe rain was one of the few safe subjects left.

He stowed the glasses in the truck and picked his hat
from the ground, flicked at it with the backs of his
fingers, releasing little dust storms. Then, turning the
hat between his hands, he squinted at the horizon.
'Every year when we wait for the first rains, everyone
is on edge. We get more drunks in town and more farm
accidents—more women pack their bags and leave
home when we're waiting for the rain. We haven't had
proper rain for three years now, so tempers are a bit—
strained.'

Emma decided this was an explanation for his insults,
if not exactly an apology. The thing was, it was no
explanation for her behaviour. What was she doing,

hitting him, even if he did richly deserve it? *She* wasn't waiting for the rain.

'Does it hurt?' she asked, as he touched his cheek again.

'Do you care?'

'Only if it doesn't.'

He laughed and put his hat on. Another long, sweeping inspection of the horizon before he looked at her. Hands on hips, he said in a more reasonable tone. 'All the same, I wish you'd go easy. Steve's impressionable and you—create quite an impression.'

Which was an improvement on the images of old B-movie sirens he'd been throwing around. Emma found she urgently wanted to dispel this image and it confused her. After all, what did it matter what the man believed? It was only for another week or so, then she'd be gone. In a month she'd be trying to remember his name.

'Look—I'm not out to seduce your brother,' she said bluntly, annoyed to be explaining herself. 'And Steve isn't losing his head over me. He just seems to welcome someone different to talk to, to confide in——'

'Confide?' The single word grated as if his throat was dry with dust and Emma blinked at the sudden blaze of anger in his eyes. 'Well, why the hell doesn't he confide in me?' He banged a fist to his chest. 'I've always been there, always——' Abruptly he broke off, breathing hard and strode away from her. Stunned, Emma shaded her eyes and stared after him. His back was poker-straight, his shoulders squared and stiff. Small puffs of dust exploded at every step he took. There was a crack as he tore a slim, dead branch from a tree and beat it on the ground as he went. After a few moments, he looked over his shoulder.

'Well? Are you coming or not?'

Emma caught up. He had himself in check now, irritable but resigned, yet that revealing snapshot of

Mackenzie, his fist pressed to his heart, pain in his green eyes, was superimposed.

'I wasn't sure you wanted company,' she said, with a throwaway gesture that doubled as fly-swatting. 'For a moment there I thought you were stomping off into the wilderness to spend some soul time alone.'

'*Soul* time?' he said with a snort.

'Well, meditation—retreat, whatever. To calm your bruised spirit.'

He glanced at her but said nothing. Maybe Mackenzie didn't admit to bruising of any kind. 'Steve said he was only seven when your parents died, so I suppose you were about——'

'Seventeen,' he said. The branch slapped on the track, dust billowed. Several tiny lizards darted to safety under a rock.

'Steve said you had just started studying environmental science and meteorology at university in Sydney when your parents were—when the accident happened.'

'Steve *has* been pouring out the family history to you, hasn't he?' he sneered.

Emma shrugged. 'You know how it is when you're romping in the hayfield.'

He stopped, gave her a baleful look then reluctantly laughed. 'Yeah, right.'

'So you gave up your studies, took over your folks' farm and looked after Steve. Wasn't there anyone else?'

'The farm was my responsibility,' he said with an air of finality. 'So was Steve.'

'What a dutiful seventeen-year-old you must have been,' she said, studying his unrevealing profile. He'd stepped into his father's shoes at a time when he probably still needed a father himself. And a mother. 'It must have been a blow, giving up your education and being lumbered with a little kid.'

He stopped and loomed over her. 'I didn't consider myself *lumbered* with my brother as you put it. I lo——' He came to an abrupt stop.

'You loved him.' She smiled brilliantly at this softer, valiantly defended side of Mackenzie. 'Steve was a very lucky boy.'

Mackenzie looked a bit off balance. 'I'm surprised you think so.'

'You would be a very comforting presence, Mackenzie, to someone whose world was collapsing around them.'

'Only then?' he said with irony. 'Let's go. I haven't got all day.'

Trailing in his wake, Emma spotted a small stone and pounced on it. Standing again, she pored over it.

Mackenzie looked back. 'Found gold?' he said in a long-suffering voice.

'Vermilion—look.' She showed him a tiny deposit of colour on the nondescript brownish-grey stone. 'I'm having a red day, so of course it caught my eye.'

Mackenzie studied her warily as if she might already have sun-stroke. 'A *red* day?'

'I do it as an exercise. It's so easy to take everything for granted, lose your ability to see small details, you know? So I often choose a colour when I wake up and then look for it all day. Something challenging, like turquoise blue on a dreary, rainy day in Sydney. Or green in the outback when there's been no good rain for years. I was having a green day when I—er—came to the fire site.' She looked up and felt the impact again of his green eyes. At least now he would know she hadn't been making a pass at him when she commented on them.

He was quizzical, not too pleased perhaps, to have his green eyes in the same category as a stone with a splash of vermilion. He cinched the brim of his hat lower, masking his eyes in a layer of deeper shadow and looked around at the baked land and scrub, mixed colours of pale red and red-brown. 'Red isn't much of a challenge out here,' he pointed out.

'No. I'm feeling idle today,' she confessed and his hoot of laughter sent two crows flapping disjointedly around a tree. Emma smiled and flipped the stone into the air, before pocketing it.

'You're saving it?' he asked.

'I collect things.'

He looked at the millions of other similar stones spread across the earth and seemed amused.

'When I get home, *my* stone will be the only one,' she said, smiling again from some sudden illogical feeling of happiness. Mackenzie looked at her curiously. They walked on.

'Now that you feel better, you can stop beating the ground with that stick,' she said, coughing at the stirred up dust.

'I'm not doing it to vent my temper,' he told her. 'I'm doing it to frighten the snake.'

Emma froze. 'The snake?' she croaked.

He turned back and took her arm, propelling her forward. She was glad of the presence of such a large alternative target and sickly aware of her bare legs. Her eyes darted everywhere, spotting minute movements on the earth that had her jumping this way and that. Mackenzie seemed quite entertained by it.

'Better switch to a green day,' he advised, looking down at her.

'Why?' she said, looking into two very good reasons.

'The snake. It's green,' he said and the sun slanted in under his hat brim, putting glints in his eyes, and she could see that he liked it a lot better, being in a category with something dangerous.

CHAPTER FIVE

THE cave was not a cave in the sense of an underground cavern but rather a hollow in the side of a rock wall, worn away by the surging of river waters over millions of years. The river had become a creek and was reduced now to a mere trickle, winding through coarse sand and rocks.

'Last century, Gertrude's grandparents had the rock gouged out and the seating made,' Mackenzie said as they bent to enter what looked like a shallow crevice. Once inside though, the ceiling suddenly soared and as the torch flashed around, Emma caught in her breath at the size of the place and the rough carved platforms in the rock, sweeping around in the sloping semi-circle that had earned the place the name 'Amphitheatre'. 'Her father had electric lighting installed early this century.' He indicated the grooves cut to bear wiring, across a spectacular column of rock that bore the ochre and black markings of aboriginal art. 'We were an insensitive lot,' he commented drily. He turned on a switch and several lights came on in the darkest recesses of the cave. 'Two descendants of the tribal people who used to use this place are on a board governing its use now. They gave us permission to use it for the centenary celebrations—which has a certain irony when you think about it.'

'It's—superb,' she said in a hushed tone. 'I had no idea.' The acoustics were amazing, the atmosphere electric. To stage a performance here was to go back to the elemental beginnings of theatre. Richard Niblett and his Travelling Troupe must have felt they'd travelled back in time. 'What a place to see theatre—

Aboriginal dance, Greek tragedy——' She flung out
her arms in enthusiasm and turned to find Mackenzie,
leaning against rugged rock, watching.

'There was an attempt a long time back to get
something started to attract a tourist trade, but it fell
through from lack of organisation and know-how,' he
said and briskly went about showing her the limits of
the lighting system. Emma inspected the 'stage', a
small area, almost centrally placed in the semi-circle of
seats. It had a level floor that was dark and almost
soundless when she stamped on it.

'Bat guava,' Mackenzie said blandly.

Emma's head came up. 'Bats?'

'They used to use this as a rookery, before the
drought. We see the occasional few, that's all. That
floor has been built up over years. The story goes that
one row of seats gets inundated every forty years.'

'Oh, terrific,' she muttered. 'My cast will just love
bats.'

But if she could just get them in here, the ambience
of the place might speak louder than the discomforts.
She mapped out some moves, consulting her script
notes then went up the slight slope and sat in the
middle of the back row of stone benches. 'Can you go
down onto the stage and say something to me,
Mackenzie? I want to check the acoustics.'

Hands on hips, he stared at her in the dim lighting.
'What would you like me to say?'

And words popped into her head, words that she
would like to hear him say to her in this dark, ancient
place in that dark, beautiful voice. She shook away the
lunacy and said lightly, 'I don't know. Let's pick a nice,
safe subject. The weather?'

Mackenzie cast her a dark look, walked down to the
stage and stood there, silent, the picture of impatience.
'Can we get this over with?'

Emma moved around to hear him from a different

vantage point. 'Will it rain, then, do you think?' she prompted in an exaggerated conversational tone.

A snort carried beautifully.

'I like rain,' she went on, moving yet again. 'As a kid I liked rainy days better than any. Put on my rubber boots and splashed through the deepest puddles. Were you a rain person, Mackenzie?'

After a few moments of silence he said, 'I was nine before I even saw rain.'

Emma stopped. 'Nine?'

'I must have seen it when I was very small but I don't remember it. From the time I was five I used to watch for it but it always seemed to rain while I was asleep.' He interspersed his sentences with pauses that gave his recitation an odd suspense. 'I'd wake up in the morning and there would be puddles, so I knew the rain had come and I'd missed it.'

Emma sat on a stone bench and propped her chin on her hands.

'Was there a drought when you were a kid?'

'Yeah.' He took off his hat and, holding it, set his hand on his hip in a pose that was both generic out here in the west, yet in the precise angle of elbow and rugged line of shoulder, distinctive to Mackenzie. 'And a flood, when I was seven. Our town—not this one— was underwater for days.'

'Well, if you saw a flood, you must have seen rain.'

He smiled. 'It rained while I was in Broken Hill, having my appendix out. When I got home, the rain had stopped and there was water everywhere. No one could understand why I was so angry about it.'

Emma couldn't remember the first time she'd seen rain. It had been one of those things in life that was always there like sunshine and heat and cold. So she had no first impression of it. She walked down toward Mackenzie, drawn by his story, the hints of him as a boy. And that voice.

'They said I should be patient. It was inevitable that I would experience rain. They tried to describe it to me. I saw it on films. . . I thought I knew what it would be like. . .' He stopped and looked at her as she came to stand beside him. 'In the end I decided it wouldn't be anything special—the way you do when you wait for something and time goes by and it doesn't happen.'

In this place, with the lovely hollow echo, it seemed to take on a significance beyond the words themselves as if he was talking about something else. 'And——' she prompted. 'When you saw it?'

'I ran outside, took off all my clothes and sang.'

Emma laughed. 'Spontaneous Matt Mackenzie. I'd like to have seen that.' But the mature Mackenzie was getting in the way of images of the child and it didn't seem like a good idea to dwell on Mackenzie, naked in the rain.

'If it hadn't already been called rain, I wouldn't have known what to name it. Some kind of magic. An enchantment.'

The words reached up and out in the cave, the perfect place for magic and enchantment.

'So—when it eventually rained—it poured?' she said, smiling at the thought of Mackenzie, overwhelmed by something.

But already the magic had dissipated and Mackenzie was squinting at the thin, white-hot line of sunlight, squeezing in at the cave's entrance and he looked sour rather than enchanted.

'A bloody deluge,' he said.

Later, on their way back to the homestead she said 'What was the song you sang in the rain?'

And Mackenzie said abruptly, 'I forget.'

'In other words, mind my own business.'

'You really are a mind-reader.'

* * *

The cloud was followed by others and moved slowly during the day, watched stoically by the locals. In the orange sunset the formations glowed prettily and when night came they made a pearly grey pattern on the indigo sky. In the morning they were gone.

But other kinds of clouds were forming. While Joyce was painting that afternoon, Bernie added a pinch of this and that to the stew she had cooking on the stove. 'I've added herbs and a good dollop of one of my best reds to your delightful stockpot, Joyce,' he told her when she came to the kitchen smeared with oil paint. He beamed, waving a glass of the same vintage. Joyce was livid.

'Oh, if it isn't the *art* expert! Well, save your best reds, mister. You might need a few stiff drinks on the last night if the bats come back!'

With this Parthian shot, she abdicated the kitchen, slammed doors right out to her beat-up Land Rover and drove off. Emma cursed silently.

'If the *bats* come back?' Bernie said ominously when the dust had settled.

So Emma told them about the cave, dwelling on its ambience, its superb theatrical potential. 'It has acoustics any actor would die for,' she said.

'Not me,' Bernie said.

'Not *underground*,' Reg told her. 'Sorry.'

'It's not in our contract,' said Alison.

The three of them elected to take the long drive into town for dinner that night in view of Joyce's walkout and they didn't invite Emma. Which left her alone in the house, her spirits at the lowest ebb in years, a headache pounding at her temples and her feet hurting. She took some painkillers, removed her shoes and phoned the theatre's lawyer to confirm that the non-disclosure of the cave as a venue meant they were entitled to withdraw. But it didn't help much. 'Oh, *damn*!' she said to Mackenzie's shelves full of journals

on cattle diseases and noxious weeds. She just knew
what *he* would say. It would have been nice to show
him that she too, could inspire personal loyalty. Emma
found she wanted to impress him. Wanted his respect.
Failure was a bitter taste in her mouth. 'Damn,' she
said again, reaching for her lighter before she remembered she'd lost it. Emma was as close to tears as she'd
been in years. To ease her stress, she went to the
abandoned kitchen and cooked a chocolate cake.

Soothed by the small chores of cleaning up and the
smell of baking, she was encouraged to go further and
mixed up dough for bread. It was a marvellously
relaxing task, the more so when she found another of
Bernie's fine reds and poured herself a glass. The
dough rose and so did her spirits. The dogs barked,
marking someone's return home. Steve, probably but
he didn't put in an appearance. Emma peeled veg-
etables to accompany Joyce's beef stew and recklessly
topped up her wine. She was singing and kneading the
bread dough one last time when someone came in. Her
heart missed a beat and made up for it with a mighty
surge. It was Mackenzie, fresh from the shower, his
hair wet and shiny, slicked back but already showing
signs of rebellion. He had a clean shirt slung over one
bare shoulder and there was a faint smudge of white
on his big chest, where he might have flung some talc
around. A tangy lemon fragrance came in with him.
All very nice, Emma thought.

'Joyce, where is everyone? And what are you cooking—it smells great,' Matt said. But Joyce wasn't there.
It was Emma standing at the big, timber table. A
barefoot Emma, wearing a green pair of the long shorts
she favoured, and a baggy T-shirt with 'Shoelace'
printed in scrawled purple script across it. She was
kneading dough and humming, flour on her face. She
raised a glass of red wine to him in salute and smiled.

'Good evening, Mackenzie.'

His mouth was open, he knew it. Emma had the dough divided into three now. He watched as she rolled each piece, stuck them together at one end then plaited them.

'Bread,' she said, noticing his interest.

Mackenzie's eyes strayed to her plaited hair. There was a spattering of flour on it where she had picked up the braid and tossed it over her shoulder in that gesture that always fascinated him, he didn't know why. 'Emma Spencer, baking bread?' he said. He looked around and saw the cake. 'Is that a chocolate cake?'

'Uh-huh. I always make a chocolate cake when I feel down.' She sent him a wide-eyed, innocent look. 'Oh, dear, the *kitchen* wasn't out of bounds too, was it?'

Matt let the shot pass, suspecting it was a diversionary tactic. 'Why do you feel down?'

She shrugged, lowered her eyes to her task. 'Oh—I don't know. The heat, the flies, the dust? And Wayne Sweet turned up at the showgrounds this morning with a massive bunch of pink carnations. Just when I thought he'd given up *adoring* me.' She sent him another wide-eyed but malicious look.

It wasn't the real reason, Matt thought. Not for the first time, he experienced an urgent wish to know just what made her sad and what made her sometimes smile that dazzling smile as if some spring of happiness suddenly bubbled up in her. Once an actress, always an actress, he thought wryly, so chances were he wouldn't find out before she went back where she belonged. And a damned good thing too. He put his shirt on. Emma glanced at him as he fastened the buttons and he felt her interest, knew that the attraction was still there for her, too. She was right when she'd told him he was greedy. He wanted her to go away, but he was pleased that she would go away wanting him. It made him feel shallow and selfish and immature, but there it was.

'I suppose you're wondering where Joyce is?' she said.

Matt started guiltily. The sight of Emma in his kitchen at the end of a long day, had knocked everything else from his mind. Dammit, when she went away it would be with him still wanting her. And that made him feel like the infatuated adolescent he'd never had the chance to be. Maybe this was a delayed, necessary phase he had to pass through on the way to true maturity, he thought in self-disgust. In another month he'd be trying to remember her name.

'Joyce—er—decided to go out,' Emma told him. 'I don't know when she'll be back but I wanted to cheer myself up so I thought I'd finish cooking the dinner.'

Emma took a pastry brush, dipped it in something and brushed haphazardly over the plaited dough, her head on one side like a kid viewing her finger-painting. 'Where is everyone?' he asked again, more disturbed now at the silence. If he didn't know better, he would think there was nobody here save himself and Emma, but of course that wasn't possible. There was always someone around.

She told him she hadn't seen Steve all afternoon. 'Joyce—decided to go out and my crew decided to—um—try one of the restaurants in Catastrophe tonight,' she said, dusting off her hands on the shorts covering her lovely backside. Another habitual gesture he had trouble with. Then she popped the bread in the oven with an ease that made him think she might bake bread often.

'This is a different image for Emma Spencer, career woman.'

'Career women have to eat.' She poured wine in a second glass and handed it to him. 'I'm an excellent cook, so don't worry.'

Matt smiled wryly. There were more important things to worry about than the quality of the food, he thought. Those legs, for instance. Those wide, womanly hips and those breasts that swayed when she moved. Matt took a mouthful of wine as she turned away to reach into a cupboard for plates. That neck with the thick braid of hair spilling curling blonde strands. How much longer was she going to be around? Matt tensely counted the days. And what the hell was keeping Steve? he thought angrily. Or Joyce. Anyone. A light sweat broke out on his brow and he frowned when Emma turned to smile at him. What the hell was she so damned light-hearted about?

He glanced at the level of the wine bottle. 'I see you're having a red day,' he said and she giggled, actually giggled. The sound was so out of character with what he knew of her, so infectious, that he laughed too. Emma's giggle turned to laughter and there they stood, laughing over nothing. She raised her glass and he raised his and the crystal clinked. 'Cheers,' she said. And when they'd taken another sip of wine they laughed again. Matt felt somehow more in danger than ever before. He should make all speed to his study and shut the door until someone came home. But there was the smell of baking bread and cooling chocolate cake and there was Emma, her grey eyes lit up with laughter, and he couldn't walk away.

No one else turned up, so they had dinner for two at one end of the big kitchen table. Mackenzie put on some music which wafted in from the living-room. After a glass of wine he began to relax and even talked to her a bit about Steve's past and his own. 'He was a bit wild as an adolescent. Got in with some rough friends and vandalised property.' He pulled a face. 'That kind of thing isn't easily lived down in the country. You aren't just another anonymous vandal the way you might be in the city. That's why I sold up the place our parents had left us and came here—to get him away from a district where everyone treated him like a troublemaker. This is superb,' he added as he buttered another chunk of crusty bread.

'Don't sound so surprised. I told you I was a good cook.'

'I suppose I thought you wouldn't be interested in things like cooking—someone with your philosophy about marriage.'

'You think women only become good cooks to please a man, Mackenzie?'

'No. But it does seem a waste otherwise,' he said provocatively.

'Chauvinist pig.'

Mackenzie laughed. Chauvinist and autocrat he undoubtedly was, but he had humour and intelligence and some very nice instincts where his brother was concerned. Libby might do worse, Emma thought, with a shaft of pure envy that cleared her head. She'd almost forgotten Libby again.

Emma told some well-worn theatre anecdotes, told him about her parents who lived in Melbourne, about her best friend Ami Winterburn whom she'd met when they were cast in a musical as twins ten years ago. 'The likeness is only superficial really—height and build and colouring. But we got to think like sisters in the end which was nice, because she's an only child like me. It can sometimes be lonely without a brother or sister.'

Mackenzie looked a bit far away as if he was checking out some horizon in his mind. 'Yes. It can be,' he said. And Emma wondered if it might be even lonelier being siblings who'd lost the feeling of family.

They compared notes on music and books. On favourite things. Flying, for Mackenzie. Walking on the beach, for Emma. 'I live near Bondi,' she explained. Safe subjects, she thought, postponing the news of trouble a little longer now that Mackenzie was mellowed and friendly. But she did tell him about Bernie's intervention in Joyce's stew and her subsequent walkout. His eyebrows went up but he saw the funny side of it. 'I won't tell either of them that the wine improved it.'

When the phone rang, Mackenzie sat for a few moments as if considering not answering it. But he merely said, 'I'll have a piece of your chocolate cake for dessert,' and went to answer the call.

Matt Mackenzie, human went out but Mackenzie, boss man came back, hands on hips, to loom over her. Emma, her mouth full of chocolate cake, savoured the last of the sweetness of the evening.

'Do you create this chaos everywhere you go?' The edges of his teeth stayed together, giving him a snarling appearance so at odds with the man willing to laugh at nothing, that Emma's first reaction was one of disappointment.

'That's a rhetorical question, I take it?' she said, standing to even things up a bit. Mackenzie moved away swiftly.

'Where the *hell* is Joyce? She's never gone on strike in the twenty-five years I've known her! All because your snobbish gourmet can't resist mincing around airing his superiority!'

The attack was unexpected, considering he'd found it quite amusing not so long before. Emma was bewildered. 'That was John Crawford on the phone. Libby's father,' he said harshly and Emma was still trying to understand how this related to Joyce when he went on.

'You had to tell, didn't you? Couldn't resist making trouble by blabbing about the night you spent in my office. Now John thinks that I—that you and I—hell! He's probably lost faith in me, and just when he most needs to——' He ground his teeth. 'And Libby is upset and taking the morning plane to Sydney. I'm going to have to drive over there and explain why I ever invited you in and how the hell we came to be sharing a bed.'

'I gave my word,' she said stiffly. 'I always keep my word. I've said nothing to anyone. Why should I?'

'The only other person who knew was Joyce and it wouldn't be her. She doesn't like Libby and she might want to sabotage my marriage but she won't if she knows what's good for her.'

'Oh, lovely. You mean she knows you could throw her out if you get miffed enough? At sixty, she could suddenly find herself homeless, with no income? Well, of course, that's one way to ensure people do what you want, *Boss*!'

He reddened. 'What the hell are you talking about?'

'Maybe Joyce doesn't feel too secure. I mean, if your child-bride objects to having good old Joyce around——'

'You know nothing about it——'

'Instead of conveniently blaming my "snobbish gourmet" for Joyce's temper tantrum today, maybe you should be asking why she's so darned on edge after twenty-five years!' Emma jabbed her index finger at his shoulder for emphasis. 'And don't tell me it's because *she's* waiting for rain, too.'

He looked fit to kill. '*Don't* presume to tell me about my own flesh and blood. Joyce had no problems till you and your pals came on the scene, and neither did I!'

'Well, here's another one. My crew won't perform in the cave so unless you can come up with something, you won't have your cave peformance for the finale.'

Mackenzie's jaw clenched. 'In that case, I see no point in your staying.'

Emma paled. 'Aren't you even going to try to negotiate? It is your committee that's at fault here, you know. The contract said——'

'I know what the contract said. But you're just too

much trouble and so are your pals. Why don't you leave? The sooner, the better.'

She felt chilled on this warm night. Another week of safe subjects with Mackenzie, she'd thought, and the idea had been both tiring and exciting. Suddenly she felt deprived.

'We'll leave in the morning, then,' she said stiffly. Her crew could drive back to Sydney but she would have to stay on in town to supervise the opening ceremony then drive home alone. Where she would stay she didn't know, but she would sleep on the showgrounds oval on bare ground rather than stay in Mackenzie's house.

'Fine,' he said.

'I don't imagine you'll be there to see us off in the morning, so I'll say goodbye now. I'd offer to shake your hand but you might humiliate me again by refusing it.' Anger at the memory made her say mockingly. 'Shall we kiss goodbye, Mackenzie?'

The air fairly crackled. The hard glitter in his eyes sent a *frisson* down her spine. It had been a stupid thing to say, a brittle, throwaway line that should have carried her offstage with her pride intact.

'Why not?' he said.

She retreated a step and her back came up against the pantry wall. Mackenzie slapped a hand on to the wall either side of her. He stooped, bringing his mouth so close to hers that she felt the ebb and flow of his breath. A pause so long that Emma thought it might never end, that she would stand here always, breathing in the scent of him, staring at his uncompromising mouth and wondering how it would feel. . . He angled his head and kissed her once, hard. It was no more than a deliberate pressure applied to a chosen spot. Mackenzie probably showed more imagination branding his cows, Emma thought, a hysterical laugh bubbling up in her. If that was all there was, she would have no trouble forgetting him. But after another pause he kissed her again, the merest brush of his mouth over hers. Her lips tingled, parted. She felt the tip of his tongue on the soft inner skin of her lips and the cool trace of him on her cheek and below her ear. It might not have happened at all, so fleeting, so delicate was the contact, but she was electrified. Mackenzie leaned back and she looked up at him, ambushed by his restraint, the controlled power in him. His green eyes turned hazy, his nostrils gently flared and he laid his hands on her hips and pulled her against him.

It was a long time since Emma had been held and never quite like this. She caught in her breath at the feel of Mackenzie's body against hers, the pleasure of his strong arms around her. In the aftermath of disillusionment she'd had no trouble keeping desire at a distance. Opportunities had offered. Handsome men, suave, sophisticated men had tried to tempt her into affairs, only to be incensed by her genuine lack of interest. Now, it was as if some missing ingredient had been supplied and she went up like a torch touched by a flame. She wound her arms around Mackenzie, revelling in the complex contours of his back, the ridges of muscle that flexed beneath her palms. Excitement ran through her, like flames licking along a powder line. He smelled so good and his body was so strong. . . Mackenzie's hands curved around her ribcage, drove upwards in an earthy little move until his thumbs teased at the soft underside of her breasts. Emma gasped and she saw the glitter of triumph in his eyes and didn't care. He flicked open a shirt button, two, and bent to put his mouth to the hollow between her breasts, peeling back the lace of her bra with small, indolent strokes of his thumbs, tracing each small exposure of skin with his mouth.

Some small sound intruded and Emma froze, abruptly aware of her gaping skirt and Mackenzie's athletic thigh inserted between hers. Her face blazed. Joyce stood in the kitchen doorway, a glint in her eyes. She looked at the slices of chocolate cake on the table. 'I see you're just having dessert,' she said blandly. 'I'll let you get on with it.'

She disappeared, banging a door loudly in the recesses of the house. Emma shakily buttoned her shirt, stunned by the strength of her desire for him, still lingering as a poignant ache low in her body. Mackenzie. In the kitchen. But if Joyce hadn't come in, they wouldn't have. . .*she* wouldn't have—would she? Emma wished she could disappear. Mackenzie muttered a curse, wiped the back of his hand across his mouth with insulting vigour. Emma felt like she'd been doused in cold water. Ice-water, she amended when he looked at her, his eyes chilling over. She was sick, humiliated.

'She won't tell,' Emma said sharply to rescue herself. 'Not if she knows what's good for her.'

Mackenzie's head went back. His hands set low on his hips.

'Goodbye, Emma,' he said in a voice dragged over gravel. 'That was the most enjoyment I've had from knowing you.'

Emma paled, for once unable to think of anything to say. To her chagrin, her mouth trembled and the tears that she'd headed off so successfully earlier, threatened again. Mackenzie's eyes flickered a bit and his shoulders bunched as if his muscles were ready to do something but his brain wouldn't let them. He turned and went out. A moment later the music stopped abruptly. In the following silence a door slammed. Then another. Outside the dogs barked then a motor started. The truck, she thought, recognising its sound now. Mackenzie, on his way to mend his reputation with his future father-in-law and wife. Libby. Emma

tidied up and viciously scraped the two slices of chocolate cake into the bin. Mackenzie, having his cake and
eating it too. She wished she hadn't forgotten
Libby again.

CHAPTER SIX

THEY left the next day in the golden haze of early morning. Emma had waited up for the others to come home from town and told them tersely that they were leaving. They were not as pleased as she had expected them to be, in fact they had seemed subdued, as if getting what they wanted had not turned out as satisfying after all. As for Emma, the taste of failure was a bitter reminder of a time when she'd made one mistake after another. Thoughts of Mackenzie and a feeling of unfinished business kept her awake until just a few hours before they left.

It was a stifling hot day with a hot wind blowing dust before it. Dry, hot and windy—ideal conditions for bushfires. A blow-up day. But there were clouds on the horizon, she noticed as they drove towards Catastrophe on their way back to Sydney. Heavy-looking storm-clouds. Mackenzie would probably be watching them somewhere through field-glasses. She saw the smoke twenty minutes from town. 'Maybe someone's burning off,' she said to Bernie who was travelling with her in the van. Maybe Mackenzie was supervising another firebreak somewhere. He had left the house before their departure. 'Up at dawn,' Joyce had said. 'A bit early even for him.'

The smell of smoke persisted. Emma felt anxious. Would a responsible person burn off in a wind like this? She stopped the van and signalled Reg and Alison in the car, to pull over. 'It might be a bushfire. I'd like to take a side road to higher ground to take a look.'

Alison cast up her eyes. 'Why, for heaven's sake? Someone else will do something if it is a fire.'

But Emma had a niggling feeling she should check it out. They had to go back half a-mile to a turn-off. It was unsealed and the smell of smoke was surpassed by the thick, cloying dust. 'Remind me to stay behind next time you get one of these Captain Marvel moods, Emma, my pet,' Bernie said into a clean white handkerchief.

When they reached the ridge, the smoke was visible against the sky. Emma checked it through binoculars, feeling foolish. Of course it would be a farmer burning off a paddock of cured grass to encourage some precious green growth for stock, or simply clearing a break around a homestead. But when she had the fire in sight, it was near no homestead.

'We'd better let Macken—someone know about this—just to be sure.'

They reported at the Bush Fire Brigade headquarters, were thanked and summarily dismissed as the alarm went out. Emma's crew had left on their journey to the city looking a bit sheepish.

'Will you be OK?' Alison asked. 'I mean, you're going to have a long drive back on your own when you've finished here.'

'I'll be fine. See you back in Sydney. Have a safe trip,' Emma said, hesitating. 'I'm sorry it didn't work out.'

The practice session at the showground was ragged and exhausting. The heat climbed from the late thirties into the forties and the sky turned a dull shade of orange as smoke drifted over the town. Near to midday, as she doggedly strode around the centre of the oval, cueing in the pom-poms, a helicopter landed on the pad alongside.

Mackenzie. Emma swallowed to encourage some moisture in her parched throat. He got out and every adult male automatically went over to him. He spoke briefly and they nodded and dispersed in a hurry, obviously with their orders. Mackenzie came over to her. Sweat ran down his face and neck and he dragged up the edge of a neckerchief to wipe it away. His eyes were narrowed against the glare and smoke.

'I hear you raised the alarm?' he said. His voice was gritty, his mouth harsh. The picture of warm gratitude, she thought, distracted by thoughts of the previous night. His eyelids flickered and he glanced at her mouth as if he, too, was momentarily diverted. 'I don't have time to say goodbye again,' he mocked.

She was already beetroot coloured from the heat but she felt an added wave of heat in her face. 'You're a brute, Mackenzie.'

'Where are your people?'

'Gone,' she said. 'Back to Sydney.'

'And left you here? They didn't waste any time,' he said derisively. 'You should have gone with them. If the fire goes the way I think it will, there won't be an opening ceremony tomorrow. There may be no celebrations at all.'

She stared at him in concern. 'Is it that bad?'

He looked at her thoughtfully. 'Low humidity, high temperatures still climbing—the fire will travel faster as the day goes on. Radiation heat is drying out the bush ahead of it, making the oils in the leaves ignite.'

'But the storm-clouds,' she said hopefully.

He smiled grimly, eyes on the clouds. 'Because of the storm-clouds there's no inversion layer to limit the oxygen available to the fire. We're likely to get spot fires when burning leaves are sucked up into the column of smoke and blown ahead to start small fires ahead of the main one.' He transferred his gaze suddenly to Emma. 'Have you seen Steve?'

Emma shook her head. 'Didn't he come home last night?'

His eyes slid away to some distant point. 'I'll send

someone to the pub to tell you if it's worth your while
to stay in town. Otherwise, you might as well hit the
road.' He hitched down the brim of his hat, whether to
better shade his eyes, or in a bushman's farewell, she
couldn't say. Whatever, it was the only hint of a
goodbye he gave before he went back to his truck.

For the next two hours Emma heard the fire reports
on the radio as she waited in the foyer of the pub. A
backfiring, to use up fuel on the fire's east flank, went
wrong and the two fires joined up. The wind had
strengthened and spot fires had started new fronts to
be extinguished. People and stock evacuated, a homestead damaged, feed crops ruined. Two volunteer
fighters taken to hospital with smoke exhaustion. A
tractor driver injured while ploughing a fire-break.
Two tourists burned when they left their car to run
from the fire. The sky over Catastrophe turned from
orange to a sullen yellowish grey.

Emma had no message from Mackenzie. But her
team came back. 'We heard how bad it was on the
radio,' Reg said. 'It sounded as if the whole place was
on fire so we came back to make sure you were OK.'

'They said on the radio that they're desperate for
more volunteers and vehicles,' Bernie said, casting a
jaundiced eye over Joyce's paintings still gracing the
pub wall. He rolled his eyes at the 'SOLD' sticker
attached to one. 'Should we lend a hand, boss?' he said
to Emma.

She blinked in surprise. 'Only if you want to. You
don't have to. It's not——'

'Not in the contract. I must have caught your Captain
Marvel mood,' Bernie sighed. He and Alison went off
to see if they could help at the community hall. Emma
and Reg went to the Bush Fire Brigade headquarters
and volunteered the van and the use of the theatre
lighting and sound equipment. It was an offer not taken
very seriously until it was clear there was a shortage of

vehicles to take food and drink to the increasing numbers of fire control posts as the wind lived up to Mackenzie's expectations.

Emma and Reg left for a post as dusk fell, kitted out with spare water and oxygen tanks and smoke masks, loaded with sandwiches and flasks of tea and coffee and a stretcher for casualties.

The sight of the theatre van, with its colourful graphics and the suddenly double-edged slogan, 'We're on our way to Catastrophe,' roused ridicule at first. 'Gee, things must be worse than I thought if they're sending in the theatre mob,' one man groaned. But, as darkness fell and volunteers were shifted around to control the spotting outbreaks, the Shoelace van with four stage spotlights rigged up on its roof came to be welcomed. In the end, as they made the journey back and forth to replenish supplies and exchange smoke-exhausted firefighters with fresh volunteers, they were being asked for by name.

'Send in the theatre mob,' someone said over the radio. 'I hear they're putting on a decent show.'

'Hear that, Mackenzie, and eat dust,' Emma said through gritted teeth, as the van bucketed along a fire trail to a new position.

He was the first person she saw at the next control camp, his bulky figure silhouetted against the glow of the firefront where other shadowy figures sprayed and raked and chopped and cleared to deny the flames anything to feed upon. She would know those shoulders anywhere, Emma thought. As their vehicle swept in, in a blaze of lights worthy of Broadway, Mackenzie glowered at them. There was no pleasing him, she decided. He looked derisive when her people left town and he looked irritated when they came back. He turned away, removed his mask and cupped his hands around his mouth to yell to someone. This was not the main body of the fire, but a small outbreak to be extinguished before it formed a new front. Even so, over its spit and crackle, Emma could barely hear Mackenzie's voice.

She and Reg did their stuff, working smoothly together the way they often had backstage. There was nothing like human efficiency to give confidence in times of danger. There was a visible brightening among the volunteers as food and drink appeared to soothe them physically and the bright lights gave them a psychological bolster in the dark broken only by the red glow of fire and their miners' torches.

Emma plugged in a lead and went over to Mackenzie with a microphone.

'What do I do with that?' he said.

'The soliloquy from *Hamlet*?' Emma mocked. 'We noticed some of your people don't have radio. You might be able to call them in for coffee and sand-wiches—do a roll call to make sure everyone is still alive and kicking, OK?'

He cleared his throat and called a few names. Two men and a woman stumbled out of the smoke haze for oxygen and sustenance. 'Gee, I thought my day had come when my name was called,' one man said, wiping his brow. 'My heart was pumping away as if I'd heard the voice of doom, or something.'

'I know exactly what you mean,' Mackenzie said, looking at Emma as he handed her the microphone. If his heart had been pumping away the day she'd called his name, it was from male outrage, nothing else.

The woman firefighter opened her coat and brought out a tiny possum. 'Mother was killed in the fire. Can you keep it safe?' Reg tucked the tiny animal into his shirt pocket.

Reg poured tea and coffee and Emma did her bit with the first-aid kit, surreptitiously watching Mackenzie as he pored over a map spread on the seat of his truck while he spoke into a radio. When he straightened, he winced. Emma went over to him with a cup of coffee and the first-aid kit.

'Is it sheer machismo that's stopping you asking for first aid, Mackenzie, or just lack of faith in me? I have a certificate, if you're worried.'

He accepted the coffee and slumped back against the truck, pushing up his smoke mast to take a gulp of the hot liquid. 'How come a theatre director has a first-aid certificate?'

'It seemed a good idea. There isn't always a doctor in the house when you want one. Where does it hurt?'

He indicated his ribs. Still drinking his coffee, he transferred his mug back and forth to unzip his firesuit and pull his arms from the sleeves. Half-naked, his skin glistening bronze as the spotlights lit him from one side, Mackenzie looked like a battered warrior—ash flecks in the hair on his chest, scratches on his arms, black smears on his face and body. Why couldn't he have a nice, straightforward leg injury? she thought crossly, looking at the broad welt and congealed blood across his ribs.

Emma laid open the first-aid kit, conscious of Mackenzie watching her every move. Just what she looked like she had no idea. But she was hot and shiny with perspiration, and stray hairs from her plait were either damply clinging to her neck or crackling with static in the dried out air. The smoke mask was stifling and uncomfortable but the alternative was worse. 'How did you do this?' she asked, indicating the injury.

'Got hit by a shovel wielded by another firefighter.' He watched Reg cheerfully serving out hot drinks and food. 'I thought you said your people had left town.'

'They had, but they came back when they heard on the radio how bad things were.' She met his gaze, childishly glad to prove that it wasn't only business that held her team together, that there was more to them all than he might have thought.

He half smiled and raised his coffee-mug in acknowledgement. Emma palpated his ribs, pressed around his back beneath his firesuit, conscious of the heat of his skin. 'I don't think anything is broken. Is that OK?'

Mackenzie's mouth tilted. 'Positively enjoyable.'

Emma eyed him with dislike. 'But not, perhaps, the *most enjoyment* you've had from knowing me?' As she knelt beside him and swabbed the wound with antiseptic, he winced. 'I apologise. I shouldn't have said that.'

Emma took the lid off a tube of salve. 'That's something, I suppose.'

'Not that it was entirely untrue—I did enjoy kissing you,' he said with a bluntness that brought the blood to her face. He tilted his head and drained the last of the coffee from the mug. 'And being kissed. Are you always such an—inventive kisser?'

Inventive! 'What do you mean *always*? If you've got some idea of theatre life as one long orgy, forget it. I haven't so much as kissed anyone for years—for at *least* a week!' But she'd mended that too late and there was a speculative gleam in his eyes. What was the matter with her? One minute she was furious that he might think her promiscuous and the next she was furious that she'd let slip she hadn't been involved with a man since Simon. Either way she couldn't win with Mackenzie. Scarlet-faced, she ripped out a length of plaster from a spool and snipped it. Then she laid it none too gently along his side.

'How was Libby?' she asked briskly. 'Did you manage to persuade her and your future father-in-law that you resisted the temptation of the theatre floozie?'

Libby's name worked like a charm, removing that reminiscent smile from his lips, bringing a look of surprise and guilt to his eyes. Was it possible, Emma thought, that Mackenzie too had forgotten Libby? She spared a thought for his predicament—committed not just to a woman he loved but to the Crawford family, if his respect and friendship with John was any guide—but attracted to a woman he didn't love. But she spared only a second of sympathy. Mackenzie might have some personal distinction and character, but he was after all just another man caught in that well-known male syndrome of wanting his cake and eating it too. Emma couldn't toss the feeling though, that it seemed too *shallow* for Mackenzie. His eyes frosted over as he saw her watching him and he slipped down his smoke-mask.

'You and Reg—stay one more hour then go back to town, take a rest,' he said.

'We're OK.'

'I'm not making polite conversation now, Emma. That's an order.'

She bristled at his tone but saluted and said, 'Yes, Boss.'

The mask tilted. 'Since when do you call me Boss?'

'Since when do you ever make polite conversation?'

He laughed softly as he plonked his helmet on his head and got on with the job. They had to change position shortly afterwards. Mackenzie shot out commands and everyone jumped to it, including Emma. When their hour was up, they headed back along the fire trail, the van carrying one volunteer suffering heat-exhaustion, a possum and a hissing, ungrateful goanna.

Day two, and small outbreaks still burned. At last, by mid-morning it seemed that the fire was being brought under control. The good news came as Reg and Emma helped a burned volunteer into the van already occupied by a terrified wallaby joey rescued from its dead mother's pouch. 'Matt says there might be a wind change which will complicate things but it's almost over,' Reg said.

'Mackenzie's here?' Emma said, looking around for him in the pall of smoke. She fancied she saw him briefly, his big shoulders hunched and his head down in a vain attempt to present a small target to the lethal radiation heat.

'Where's the joey?' Reg asked from inside the van. 'It's escaped——'

'I'll get it,' Emma said, spotting the tiny creature as it hopped into scrub. 'You finish loading the stuff in and start the van up.'

'Hey, Boss. Maybe you shouldn't——' Reg yelled after her, but she was running, breathing wheezily through her smoke mask.

'Here, joey, joey——' she called ridiculously, feeling light in the head. Somewhere a siren was sounding but she didn't dare take her eyes off the spot where the animal had disappeared. 'Here, wallaby——' Treading carefully so as not to alarm the creature, she followed and pounced on it.

'Emma!' someone yelled behind her. 'Answer me!'

'Here,' she said. The wallaby resisted and dug sharp claws into her shoulder and, eyes watering, she turned towards the voice that she knew was Mackenzie's. He crashed through the undergrowth to her, in full fire-fighting gear now, with a water tank on his back. 'What the hell are you doing? Are you mad?'

'Rhetorical questions, right?' she croaked, hearing suddenly the increased roar of the fire. Mackenzie grasped her arm and hauled her through the bush.

'The wind just changed,' he bit out. 'We've got to get out of here before——'

His words broke off on a sharp intake of breath. Emma catapulted into his backpack as he stopped abruptly. When she raised her head it was to the most terrifying sight of her life. The trees ahead were alight and the fire had crowned, boiling along the treetops spitting out burning leaves and twigs to propagate itself in the dry grass below. With Mackenzie, Emma turned to look behind them. Her mouth went dry. They were surrounded by flames.

The radiation was unbearable. Emma felt her skin searing. Panic tore at her and she swallowed hard to prevent herself from screaming. Mackenzie ripped off his helmet and put it on her head. She looked into his eyes and saw the grim confirmation there of their plight. He sprayed water over them both, soaking them.

'The fire is a thin line there——' he said, pointing. Through the groundfire she could see blackened earth and the flickering figures of firefighters spraying and beating at flames, their mouths opening and shutting in silent shouts. Looking hard at her Mackenzie said clearly. 'We can run through it to ground that's already been burned. You'll have to let go of the wallaby, Emma——'

She closed her eyes momentarily. Run through fire? It went against every natural instinct, even when the alternative was so dreadful. But Mackenzie was with her. 'I can't,' she croaked.

'Yes, you bloody can!' he said explosively.

'No, no—I meant I can't leave the wallaby,' she clarified and swung away, possessively clutching it when he tried to remove it. 'I killed that kangaroo on the road, you see, so——' Mackenzie rolled his eyes, but didn't seem to find this explanation irrelevant. 'I wasn't going to leave it to fry!' he yelled. 'But *I'll* carry it.' He grabbed the creature, shoved it inside his overalls, swearing. 'Run double over and don't breathe in. When you're through the flames fall down and roll. They'll spray us on the other side. Ready?'

'Mackenzie——' she croaked, staring at him, wanting to say something meaningful but she didn't know what. She thought she should know at a moment like this, exactly what she felt for him. 'What did you sing in the rain?'

And he made a sound somewhere between a growl

and a laugh, pulled her to him and told her then kissed
her hard on the mouth.

'Now!' he bawled, and they steeled themselves and
ran into the fire.

CHAPTER SEVEN

THE stars were veiled by smoke. Emma sat on the veranda at Falkner's Place and gazed at the sky, catching a glitter here or there as the haze slipped by. The fire was all but extinguished and in the hands of the professionals. The volunteers had gone home, a few to rescue what they could of stock and memories from burned out homes and land. Falkner's Place had suffered some singed paddocks but no real damage.

It was after midnight and everyone was asleep except Emma. She had dozed off but woken with visions of a towering fire, the burned patch on her forearm stinging. Vaguely she remembered emerging from the flames with Mackenzie, rolling on hard ground, the feel of rain on her. It was water from the fire hoses, of course, but Emma had sung 'Rain, rain, go away' as she was led to a stretcher. She had been in shock, she was told at the tiny district hospital. All her skin was pink and tingling from the radiation heat but thanks to Mackenzie she walked out of the hospital later that day, suffering only the after-effects of smoke inhalation and burns to one hand.

Catastrophe had lost some of its outlying houses and the community hall had been damaged when the wind had carried some burning debris and dropped it under its timber stairs. Emma had found Bernie with Joyce, cleaning up in a church hall where they had been cooking for the evacuated kids.

'Sausages and mash,' Joyce said with satisfaction. 'It turns out the galloping gourmet here used to be a short-order cook in a café.'

Bernie looked around with a pained expression.

'Starving actors can't be choosy, but please! I have my image to think of.' Joyce just gave her rusty laugh and slapped him on the back.

Alison, made up as a cat, was tidying up the theatre make-up kit. Several children, made up as mice, clustered around her, waiting to be collected by parents. 'Had to distract them somehow. If there's anything I can't stand, its squalling kids,' she said. 'I'm dying for a cigarette.'

It had seemed perfectly natural for them to come back to Falkner's Place with Joyce. Only two days since they'd driven away with the feeling of unfinished business. Back here, star-gazing through the smoky haze, Emma still had the feeling.

In the dense silence she heard the flick of a light switch and a rustle of movement. She went inside to see who was keeping her company in insomnia. A light was on in Mackenzie's study.

His back was to the door as he leaned against a high cabinet, chin in hand, looking at something. He wore frayed shorts and a sleeveless T-shirt that had seen better days, as he had. His left wrist was bandaged and his hair was singed. There was cuts and scratches on his arms and legs. Never the loveliest of men, he now looked a mess. Yet Emma found a distinct pleasure in looking at him. It might be the first time, she realised, that she'd ever caught him unawares. Mackenzie always saw her first and was always ready for her and so never revealed much. She looked at his long, muscular legs and bare feet. For once Mackenzie was revealing plenty. She smiled, enjoying the rugged line of his shoulder and biceps as he hitched his hand low on his hips, following slavishly the tug of fabric and flex of muscle across his back. All genuine working muscle, she thought, thinking of the gym-built bodies she saw regularly. Very nice in their way, but glossy, show-pony stuff compared to Mackenzie's powerful frame. She was caught up in admiration and an odd feeling of tenderness for him.

He straightened and abruptly turned. His eyes shifted over her, lingering on her white silk robe and she saw his unguarded response to her and felt the sting of heat on her skin and a primitive sense of triumph.

'I couldn't sleep,' she said huskily.

'Same here.' Mackenzie didn't move, just kept looking at her. At length he walked away and as he passed his desk, he dropped something in it, pushed the drawer shut again. It only half closed and Mackenzie looked uncharacteristically hesitant as he glanced back at it. 'Drink?' He opened a drinks cabinet and poured two measures of Scotch over ice, added soda.

'How are your burns?' he asked, as he gave her the drink.

'Stinging. How are yours?'

He grinned. 'The same. I lost some hair.' He ran his hand ruefully over the long and the short of it.

'I haven't thanked you,' she said. 'If you hadn't come looking for me, I wouldn't be here now. My carelessness put you in danger too. I'm sorry.'

'No apologies necessary. Or thanks. I was only doing my job,' Mackenzie said, taking a mouthful of his drink.

His tone was prosaic, heading off any intimacy that might evolve even from gratitude. Emma's pulse-rate slowed. She had probably been mistaken about the electricity in the air. It was very likely just static in this dry weather. 'Well, thank you for doing it well enough to save my life.'

'Don't make a big deal out of it, Emma.'

'Sorry. It's just that I think not being burned to death *is* a big deal.'

He laughed, ran a hand over his head once more and took a quick slug of his drink. All this hesitancy and repetitive gestures—anyone would think he was nervous, Emma thought. Possibly delayed reaction. After he'd jumped through a wall of flame with her, he'd gone straight back to help contain the last of the fire outbreaks. He sat on the edge of his desk and Emma propped herself against the cabinet that was still warm where he'd leaned on it. Idly, she glanced at a chart lying there. It was the one with red stickers she'd seen a long time ago in his town office. Not quite a week. Half a lifetime, it seemed. A red felt pen lay beside it. Emma peered at the chart and noticed a red dot inked in beside Catastrophe. 'What does that mean?' she asked, but of course as soon as she said it she knew. 'Oh, it must be the bushfire you've marked——' And it was a logical step then to assume that the other red stickers marked other fires. 'All these were fires?' She frowned, remembering someone telling her there had been an outbreak of bushfires. 'We were in these towns on tour and I don't remember ever seeing smoke——'

He removed the chart and stood it facing the wall, the way he had that other night.

Emma stared at its blank flipside, hearing the echo of her last words. We were in these towns on tour. . . And now, while they were at Catastrophe, a fire here too. Her eyes went to Mackenzie. She remembered the intense way he'd looked at her in his office that other time. What had she said? 'We didn't exactly set those towns on fire.' But of course, it had been a joke about poor attendance for their show. A figure of speech. Now he folded his arms and looked broodingly at her.

'You don't think——?' she began, then laughed. 'Of course not. You couldn't think the two things are linked—us and the fires. . .'

He said nothing. Emma snatched up the chart and looked again. 'Were you marking our progress?' she'd joked. The fires marched alongside the route they'd taken, practically to Mackenzie's front door. She laughed scratchily. 'Well, I know you think we're a careless lot but you can't think we started them all with cigarette butts. That would be too coincidental.' Her eyes widened, searched his carefully expressionless face. 'Too coincidental,' she repeated. 'Does anyone know how those fires started, Mackenzie?' she asked hoarsely.

'It seems fairly certain they were deliberately set.'

Emma caught in her breath. 'Deliberately——' She started at him, shocked by the idea. Carelessness would have been too coincidental; arson was a different matter. 'But that's—that's ludicrous!' she said, giving a cracked laugh. 'We're a theatre group.'

'Everywhere you went there's been a fire.'

'Not until we got to here!' she stabbed a finger at the town marked with the first of the outbreaks. 'If one of us is a—a firebug, why wait till here to light up?'

'That's the start of the drought area,' he said with a shrug. 'Drier fuel, higher temperature—good country for setting fires. The conditions make it difficult to be absolutely certain of arson. Almost irresistible to a firebug.'

'You can't seriously believe that one of us is responsible! Come on—which one? Bernie? The nearest he gets to a flame is to flambé something. Alison? The only fire she needs is the one on the end of a cigarette—she might start something by accident, but not *four*. Reg? Reg is an absolute softie about wildlife; he couldn't do it.'

Still he looked steadily at her. Emma blinked. The blood drained from her face. 'Me?' she said at last and gave a crack of laughter. She was humiliated, horrified that she hadn't seen it coming. 'You can't suspect me?'

'You carry that lighter,' he said evenly, very detached, like someone giving evidence and striving to be fair. She felt like hitting him. 'You insisted on

coming out to the firebreak site with me that night.
You kept tossing that lighter, watching it.'

'Dear me. That's conclusive. What else exposed my
secret life as a pyromaniac?' she drawled.

'You were in the stables with a naked flames holding
it near highly flammable material—to find your torch,
you said. Your torch never did show up.'

She gaped at him, remembering the way he'd taken
the lighter from her. Later he'd dropped it and subsequent searches had never turned it up. And her luck,
she thought, just kept getting worse and worse. 'You
think I didn't have a torch at all? It was there, I found
it the next morning,' she said hotly.

Mackenzie didn't answer. But of course, he only had
her word for it that she'd had a torch and found it
again. Emma took a turn about the study in frustration,
impatiently dragging her robe free when the sleeve
caught on a desk drawer handle. The implicatons hit
her suddenly, like a giant hammer blow.

'You thought I was about to set fire to the stables?
Stables, full of horses?' she whispered, so wounded
that he could imagine her capable of inflicting pain on
innocent creatures that she lashed out at him, catching
his upper arm with her open palm. 'You think I'd let
those poor, unsuspecting animals be burned to a crisp?
You think I was going to lurk somewhere watching—
that's why pyromaniacs do, don't they? Stay to enjoy
their own handiwork?' Tears of rage stood in her eyes
and she could barely see him. If she could have yelled,
she would have but the house was deathly quiet and
her rage and hurt were expressed in a low, savage voice
that gathered speed and resonance. 'What kind of
monster do you think I am, Mackenzie?' She clenched
her fist and threw a punch at his face. He ducked it,
grabbed her wrists and held her off, not without a
struggle. Emma's strength was buoyed by rage and a
terrible disappointment but he was built like a rock and

all her silent struggles and barefooted kicks couldn't shift him.

'I didn't accuse you,' he said abruptly.

'Like hell you didn't!'

'I merely pointed out that the facts lend themselves to certain—theories.'

'Your theory has holes in it,' she snapped. 'I was the one who pointed out that those red marks followed our itinerary, that night in your office. Why would I do that if I was implicated? And how could I make jokes about something that might mean discovery?'

'You're an actress,' he pointed out, eyes narrowed on her. His muscles flexed to contain her angry surge. And of course, she thought bitterly, thrill-seekers often drew attention to themselves—it was part of their weakness.

'Emma—those fires were deliberately started, that's all anyone knows. I have a half-baked theory that's keeping me awake at night——' he said cryptically. 'Eventually, there'll have to be an investigation and I'm going to have to report for the Brigade and by rights I should give them that chart and any information——'

'Can I expect the arson squad to *interrogate* me, Mackenzie?' she spat.

'Look—are you listening to me?' he said harshly. 'This is between you and me. It never would have come up if you hadn't crept around in the middle of the night, spying on me. I haven't said anything to anyone about it. Nobody but you and I have seen this damned chart.'

Emma thrust her face close to his. 'And it had better stay that way, Mackenzie. If you cast a slur on my reputation, or the theatre's, I'll sue you for defamation.'

'How come you show business people are so fond of litigation, Emma?' he said and she was incensed at the

wry note of amusement in his voice. His hands eased a
little on her arms and she felt the slide of his fingertips
through the silky fabric. There should have been no
way she could respond to that, not after what had just
been said and not said. Yet her skin tingled and she
was abruptly aware of her body and its cravings. She
experienced a rush of adrenalin. Or something. For
what seemed like minutes she stood there, as immobile
as he, reading the desire in his eyes and in her own
heart. Unfinished business, she'd thought when she'd
driven away two days ago.

'I—um——' she whispered, trying to remember what
the question had been.

Mackenzie's eyes glittered. 'It was a rhetorical question,' he said.

Emma's senses were heightened. Somewhere in the
house old timber creaked. Outside the vast silence was
broken only by the small, soughing sounds of a breeze
and the tender rattle of olive leaves. Even that stopped
and Emma heard the sound of her own heartbeat and
the tiny popping sounds of effervescence in the drinks,
scarcely touched, on the desk. In the air was the
lingering smell of smoke that she feared might never
go away again and the warm, astringent scent of
Mackenzie's skin that surely would.

'You hair didn't burn,' he said softly. His voice was
hoarse from smoke and shouting and had a new,
mellowed quality, a rich huskiness that rippled along
her skin as if she was receiving the voice impulses as a
tactile, not an aural sense. Like the rub of raw silk. It
took her a moment to realise that Mackenzie was
actually touching her as well, his fingers spread and
combing through her hair, letting out the last of the
braiding. He gathered up handfuls of the loosened hair
and stared at it.

'I wondered what it would feel like in my hands—
when you came out of my shower that first night——'

His hand touched her cheek and she turned her face into the touch. 'I thought *you* might have been bald, under your helmet, when I first saw you,' she said. 'And sagging under your clothes.' She touched his shoulders, traced her fingertips over the beautiful upper arms she'd admired.

His eyes glinted as he drew her against him, so that she felt the imprint of him from thigh to breast. She drew in her breath sharply as he placed a hand on her lower back and tipped her closer still. Nothing sagging about him at all. Just the reverse.

He walked away then, abruptly and she spun around, dazed and disconsolate, a protest on her lips. Emma stared at him, thinking that she would plead, probably, to be close to him again, feel his arms around her. The thought widened her eyes, put a sheen on her lips, and he stood a moment watching her, then closed the door. 'You didn't think I was leaving?' he said ironically, catching her close. He sat on the edge of his desk and drew her with him, holding her in a pincer movement of his thighs as he nuzzled into her neck. 'I couldn't leave if I wanted to——' he said indistinctly against her skin. He traced the edges of her robe down to her waist and untied the belt. The robe slipped open and Emma tensed, conscious as always of her over-abundance, but when Mackenzie's large, calloused hands cradled her breasts the sheer sensual response of her body drove all else from her consciousness. Mackenzie stooped and drew the tip of a breast into his mouth and sucked, a piercing sweetness so intense, so tangible that it shot through her, anchoring her to the floor. She held hard to his thighs either side of her and let her head drop back, her body held and supported by Mackenzie as he pleasured her. 'Mackenzie,' she said on a sigh.

'Will you ever call me Matt?' he said, raising his head. He lifted her breasts, fondled, stroked in tiny, teasing circles with his thumbs.

'Matt. Matthew. Mackenzie,' she said, her voice catching as he punctuated her speech with calculated moves of his hands and laughed and she could see his satisfaction in the power he had to please her. But she had power too. She caressed him, delighted in the muscular hollows and contours of his back, slid her hands beneath his T-shirt to explore his chest and muscle-ridged midriff. With exquisite anticipation she leaned in close and kissed the junction of his shoulder and neck, tracing the tip of her tongue on his skin, smiling at his responding tremor. She moved against him, with him, until the sensuality of touching him seemed indistinguishable from the sensuality of being touched by him. Mackenzie muttered something and dragged his shirt off over his head. Through half-closed eyes she watched the powerful stretch of his upper body.

'You're a beautiful man,' she said huskily, not waiting for him to rid himself of the shirt before she bent and brushed her mouth over his chest. She pushed her hands to the top of his thighs and centred them over his shorts, catching in her breath at the size and strength of him. Mackenzie's body jolted as if he'd had an electric shock. He fought his way out of the T-shirt and tossed it on the floor and Emma ran fingertips over his shoulders, down over the lovely, bulging contours of biceps and lightly over his chest, circling his cuts and bruises. Sheer indulgence. Emma smiled, watching her hands on him, enjoying the pleasure of touching and the sweet sting of anticipation as he slid her robe from her shoulders. The silk slithered to the ground and she stood there before him in black satin briefs, her hands tentatively at her breasts now that she had no illusion of cover.

'Emma, you're magnificent,' he breathed and planted a kiss on her neck.

She unfastened the button of his shorts waistband,

enjoying his sharp, indrawn breath and the stain of colour in his face. It was as if she'd been waiting all her life to feel so free, so uninhibited. She'd run through fire with him and now there was nothing she could not do with him. As he unzipped his shorts, she walked around the desk to turn the lamp aside. 'The light's in my eyes,' she explained, aware that he watched every move of the body that had often embarrassed her with its plenitude. Now, she slowed down her walk, elated at the effect she had on him. At her touch, the light shifted across Mackenzie like a spotlight, then passed on, throwing him into chiaroscuro, his skin gleaming bronze, his powerful musculature sculpted in shadow. As she moved irresistibly towards him, she bumped into the half-open desk drawer and, glancing impatiently at it, shut it. But her eye retained an image, a gleam of gold, and she pulled the drawer open again. Her gold lighter lay there.

Emma smiled languidly. 'My lucky charm,' she said huskily, taking it out. 'I was beginning to think one of your horses had swallowed it.' One more step towards him then she frowned. How long had this been in his desk? She looked down at the lighter, turned it over and over in her palm, feeling only a dull echo of the pleasure its restoration should have given her.

'I've searched the stables for this. . . How long have you had it?'

He set his hands on his hips. Head lowered, he looked up under creased brows. 'I was intending to send it to you——'

'Oh, really?'

His mouth compressed at her tone. 'One of the men found it in the stables the morning you left here. . . I would have told you except that the small matter of a wildfire distracted me.'

'But you'd remembered it tonight,' she said. This was what he had dropped in the drawer when she came in. 'Were you looking at it along with your fire chart and drawing some conclusions? Was this,' she raised the lighter and her hand shook slightly, 'Was this to be Exhibit A?'

'I was looking at it,' he said heavily, 'And wondering if you were still awake—and if I could possibly use it as an excuse to come to your room.'

Emma blinked. 'Oh.' Any pleasure she might have had in this boyish scenario was killed off by his tone. He despised himself for wondering about her and seeking excuses to see her in the middle of the night. Despised himself for wanting her. Emma's skin chilled. And he probably despised her too, for having the power to make him plot and plan like a schoolboy.

Her nakedness was suddenly a cold and embarrassing thing. She crossed her arms over her breasts. Mackenzie gave a lopsided smile and stood there, his weight thrown on to one leg, hands low on his hips, clad only in his briefs. The soft lamplight emphasised the pure masculinity of form, the beauty of his chest and shoulders, expanded in the pose, the dynamic power of calf and thigh muscles. Yet he could deliver a caress as if it was a feather he trailed across her skin. And his mouth, so tough and set in irony, could be tender. Her body responded to the memory. As she looked at him, feeling the pressure of her own arms across her breasts, she thought of his hands there instead, his mouth. She thought of the pleasures still to explore. . .of lying with him, taking that magnificent body into hers. She experienced a sharp pang of desire and regret. For she knew if she said the word, Mackenzie would come to her and put those fabulous arms around her and make love and he would be superb, she knew it, and her body clamoured for him.

He waited, saying nothing, for dressed as he was he had no need to say that he hadn't changed his mind. But Emma couldn't say the word. She disliked that taint of self-contempt in him. It was a hollow triumph to have got beneath Mackenzie's self-control and made him want her when he knew he shouldn't. Because she'd remembered Libby. Mackenzie hadn't changed his mind about Libby, either. Libby was the fresh young country wife to be, and this startling chemistry between Mackenzie and herself was a passing danger, like the fire — to be extinguished before getting back to real life. But she had no intention of becoming Mackenzie's guilty secret. Her self-esteem quailed at how nearly she had been just that.

She seized her wrap from the floor and turned her back to put it on, tying the belt with a decisive knot. Her face was flushed. How could she have been so uninhibited? Belatedly, she felt all the embarrassment she ever had about her over-abundance. She must have looked like some cheap imitation of a Sixties movie queen, poncing about, wiggling her hips, her breasts bouncing. Emma scowled. But if she hadn't been moved to flaunt herself, she wouldn't have seen the lighter in the drawer and been reminded that Mackenzie thought of her as trouble.

'I take it the mood has flown,' Mackenzie said.

She turned, annoyed by the lazy, mocking voice. 'I wouldn't want you to hate yourself in the morning,' she said distinctly.

His eyes flickered at that. It always annoyed him when she guessed what he was thinking. Emma felt no satisfaction at being right, this time.

'Goodnight, Mackenzie.'

'Goodnight, Emma,' he said and she fled the sound of that dark-timbred voice.

'Matt and the men are going out to fix up a few places today,' Joyce told Emma, when she emerged from her bedroom the next morning. 'You know — cover in shattered windows, put tarpaulins over damaged roofs—you never know when it might rain.' She gave a cracked laugh. The storm-clouds had not brought rain to Catastrophe but fifty miles away, when the temperature was a scorching forty-six degrees Celsius hailstones had punched holes in a roof and killed poultry. 'Tea, coffee and muffins in the kitchen if you want breakfast.'

There was more than that in the kitchen. Mackenzie was there, and clinging to him was Libby.

'Thank goodness you're all in one piece, Matt,' she was saying. Her hands moved over his chest, seeking reassurance of his wholeness. She transferred them to his neck. 'I was so worried. I would have come back from Sydney sooner but couldn't get a flight. I could have helped Dad—he had so much to do and he looks so sick——'

'It was a rough couple of days. We all look sick, kitten,' he said and gave her waist a squeeze. Libby's hands wandered over his shoulders and down his arms then started on his chest again. Surely by now she had established he was in one piece, Emma thought sourly. This was sheer indulgence. She hated herself for knowing exactly how addictive it could be. Over Libby's head, she met Mackenzie's gaze. He was embarrassed that this affectionate scene was being witnessed by a woman he'd almost bedded the night before, she could see, but he got it quickly under control. Only Emma's training stopped her from turning tail. Libby looked around, and said coolly, 'Oh, hello. I hear you've been quite helpful with the fire. Thank you.'

It might have been genuinely meant but Emma felt she'd been reminded once again that she was an outsider. The sight of Mackenzie with Libby in his arms was hardly necessary to ram the message home. Last night belonged with the wildfire and emergencies. People did strange things in emergencies. But afterwards they wanted to get back to normal, tidy things up, put everything back in its proper place.

And her proper place was not here. Mackenzie gently set Libby aside and said, 'Could I see you in my office, Emma? The celebrations are cancelled, of course, but we have some unfinished business.'

She quailed at the phrase but preceded him into his study.

'There isn't anything outstanding we have to discuss, Mackenzie,' she said, trying not to look at the desk or the carpet across which she'd minced, making a prize fool of herself.

'About last night——' he said. He went to the window, stared out, hands on hips, as if nothing about the outside world met with his approval. 'The circumstances are very—there are things that I——' He turned back to her, bit into his lower lip with big, strong teeth. 'When will you leave?'

She paled angrily at his undisguised anxiety to get rid of her. Last night's folly. Emma took some deep, controlled breaths and made a reasonable job of sounding relaxed. 'We need to check out our vehicles, especially the van. Is tomorrow morning soon enough?'

His eyes flickered. 'Emma—I should explain——'

She held up her hand. 'No need to explain, Mackenzie. Let's not make too much of it. These things happen from time to time—especially in times of stress and shock.'

His mouth compressed. 'Do they?'

She waved a hand, getting into the spirit of it now, knowing what she sounded like. The mythical, sexually free woman who took her pleasure and moved on, no strings, no emotional hangovers. The kind he seemed to assume she was, from the start. Emma felt the recoil of distaste for it, but it let her leave with her pride intact. 'It's been quite a week, crowned by a little midnight madness. So what?'

'It would have been midnight-to-dawn madness if

you hadn't found your lucky talisman just when you did,' he pointed out sardonically.

Emma faltered in confusion at the reminder. Her eyes shifted to the desk and he caught the movement with satisfaction. 'We were quite creative, weren't we?' he said softly.

The bastard. Emma looked at him in dislike and remembered telling him that he was a beautiful man. That proved it really was madness. The man was built like a stolid monument without an ounce of grace, and his manner matched. But she smiled, with a touch of fondness such as a sexually liberated woman might feel for a talented lover. It seemed to irritate him. 'I certainly have no regrets,' she lied. 'Either that we started or that we stopped when we did.'

'Oh, good.' He took up his hat and put it on. Emma stared in fascination as he crushed it on to his head with a slamming blow of one large hand. He made a mocking little gesture for her to precede him from the room and followed, banging the door behind him.

Bernie and the others studied Mackenzie's face with interest as the boss man strode through the house and went out, slamming another door.

'If I put on some speed, we could be ready to leave today,' Reg said diffidently.

There were no objections to the idea. Everyone, including Alison and Bernie, helped get the vehicles ready. Emma packed up her few things in the bedroom, keen to leave but depressed about it. She paused in front of the mirror to rebraid her hair ready for the journey when the door opened. Her heart bounded into a fast rhythm before she saw that it was Libby. What had she expected? Mackenzie?

Libby smiled. She wore a designer jumpsuit and superb tan leather ankle boots. Several dress rings glittered on her hands and half a dozen gold bangles softly jingled on her wrist. She moved around the room, running a finger along the mahogany of an antique dresser, touching the tassels on the curtain cords.

'He will marry me, you know,' she said at last, making eye contact with Emma's mirror image. 'I wouldn't want you to go away thinking that he might change his mind.'

Emma raised her brows politely. 'Are we talking about Mackenzie?'

'I heard about you and Matt sleeping together at his office.'

Emma felt hot and flustered confronted with this cool young thing. 'How *did* you hear about that?'

'Joyce told a friend of mine. And my friend just couldn't *wait* to tell me,' Libby said, wrinkling her nose.

Emma reflected that Joyce didn't, after all, know what was good for her. 'Nothing happened. We shared a divan, that's all.'

'Oh, I'm not worried about that. We're not engaged yet and it doesn't bother me if he has one last fling.'

Emma winced.

Libby moved closer, still touching the furniture, putting her mark on everything. Unnecessary, Emma thought. When she married Mackenzie, it would all be hers.

'There's something between you and Matt. I saw it straight away. It isn't so surprising. You're more his age. You run your own show, as Matt does, and he respects competent people.'

If Mackenzie grouped her with the competent people he respected, it was the first Emma had heard of it.

'And you're beautiful, I suppose, in a way.'

Damned with faint praise, Emma thought. 'You're not exactly a hag yourself,' she said.

Libby looked at herself in the mirror. 'Oh, I know what I've got going for me. I know what goes into running a place like this; I know how to organise a house like this and work on committees and I understand men like Matt. He's a lot like my father.'

Emma blinked at this, wondering how Mackenzie would like being likened to his intended's daddy.

'I'm the perfect wife for a man like Matt. That's what I was raised for. I couldn't do anything else even if I wanted to.'

Some vague note of discontent prompted Emma to say, curiously, 'And do you want to?'

'Being Mrs Mackenzie will be more than enough for me,' she said rather snappily. 'As big a challenge as running a theatre—more, maybe.' She seemed quite annoyed about it. Emma felt Libby's glare as she bent her head to flip the completed braid over her shoulder. She snapped an elastic band around it. 'Of course, I'm at a disadvantage just at present because Matt won't make love to me,' Libby said frankly.

The rubber band sprang from Emma's fingers and she knelt down to feel around on the floor for it. Libby, too, got down and searched. She went on conversationally, 'I expect Dad's got some kind of understanding with him—you know what fathers are like. He wouldn't be very happy with any man taking me to bed and Matt's been good friends with Dad since he moved here, so——' she shrugged.

Emma looked at her aghast. 'You mean your father might have told Mackenzie not to—um——'

'I've found it.' Libby handed her the rubber band and they got up from the floor. 'Not *told* exactly, I wouldn't think. An unspoken thing—men have this kind of *code*. Matt always tells me I'm too young and we'll wait until we're engaged. Which is annoying because I'm not quite the innocent they think and Matt is very—very—attractive.'

Emma felt a shaft of pure jealousy. Which was probably what Libby intended. She couldn't believe that the girl was really so artless and confiding. This time she got the elastic band on and tucked a few stray ends away.

'I just thought I'd tell you,' Libby said. 'In case all that firefighting you did with Matt has given you ideas.'

'It hasn't,' Emma said crisply.

'Because, you see, Matt's a bit old-fashioned. Dad says he's a man of honour in a dishonourable age. Even if Matt had changed his mind, he'd never in a million years back down from a commitment. And he's committed to me.'

Emma gathered up her clothes, some still smelling of smoke, and stuffed them into her bag. This was her punishment for last night's folly. Having this bright, complacent young thing trilling on about Mackenzie as a husband and lover, warning her off. It struck Emma that she had been warned off such a lot since coming to Catastrophe.

'Better make sure he's really what *you* want then, before the wedding,' Emma said drily. 'A man who wouldn't back down on a commitment in a million years probably wouldn't ever let a wife go—even if she wanted to.' She regretted her sardonic repetition of Libby's own phrase. It was a cheap shot. 'But I hope you'll be very happy,' she added stiffly.

Joyce had prepared some food for them to take. 'No chocolate cake,' she said straight-faced, to Emma. 'For a while there I had high hopes for you and the Boss. I can't believe he can be serious about spending his life with someone who answers to 'kitten'. Can I come and visit you in town?'

Taken aback, Emma said yes, but she felt a faint uneasiness at the idea of any overlap between her life in the city and this mad interlude here.

'You lot turned out to be the genuine thing. I reckon they should give you an award, or the keys to the town,' Joyce said with a wink. 'For what that's worth.'

Emma laughed. The keys to Catastrophe. It was so ironic, she was still laughing as she drove the van away from Falkner's Place. There was hardly anyone around as they drove past Col Mundy's pub and the blackened community hall with its poster still advertising their comedy. One woman came out of a shop to wave them goodbye. Other than that, the only movement on the streets of Catastrophe was the flutter of a few remaining flags. In the rear-view mirror, Emma's eyes lingered on a lime one. Today, without making a conscious choice, she was having a green day.

CHAPTER EIGHT

SHE was home. Emma took in great gulps of air, filled with fumes and pollutants and sea-salt, the scent of Sydney. She felt a great wave of nostalgia. The drum-roll of traffic, the hoots of cars and buses and ferries, the screech of brakes. Familiar, maddening music that rose and diminished but never switched off. Emma aired her house and went shopping, doing battle with other drivers for a parking space, duelling with trollies in a supermarket. She had a haircut and worked out at the gym, and lay indolently, drink in hand on her deck while the sun set over Sydney's red-tiled roofs, striking reflections off the dust particles that hung over the city, in glorious pink and orange. Home, she thought, sipping tomato juice and loving the noisy, ugly, beautiful, breathtaking, lung-scorching mess that humanity had built.

Yet it wasn't the same. Emma sat there, watching the sunlight fade, aware of divided loyalties. A part of her held another image of home—a wide, empty, silent place under an immense blue sky. A place scarred and wrinkled by time, where people waited for what they wanted, knowing that nothing could hurry the crops or the birth of lambs or the rain. Motionless, she sat, in a way she never could have once, watching the sun disappear over the horizon prickled with palm-trees and towers and office blocks. The country had got to her. Mackenzie's country. Mackenzie.

Days passed. She tore into the work that had piled up in her absence. At Ami's insistence she called in at her theatre supplies shop for a report on the successful drama project and to check out a new range of colour palettes.

'Fantastic bruise effects,' Ami said, in a selling mood. She already bore a realistic bruise on her cheekbones and a congealed stab wound on her hand, demonstration pieces for customers. 'What about a nice knife-wound, or an abrasion?' she tempted, but looked more closely at her friend. 'Coffee. Tell me all about him.'

Emma laughed. 'I knew you'd be intrigued. Well, he really *was* an Adonis—black, curling hair, sooty eyelashes and Mediterranean blue eyes——'

Ami waved dismissal of Mediterranean eyes. 'Not him. Seen one Adonis, seen them all. The other one. The MCP. The Boss.'

Emma pulled a face, casually picked up a make-up brochure. 'Oh, him. You know the type—all muscle and machismo. No looks to speak of—his brother got all the good looks.' She flicked a page and it made a sharp sound. 'One of those big, overbearing, patronising, arrogant——' another page flicked '—bristly brutes.'

'My intuition is working overtime,' Ami said, as she set two cups of coffee down, 'No redeeming features for this male chauvinist?'

Green eyes. A voice to send shivers down your back. Strong arms that could be gentle. Sex appeal that just stopped her in her tracks. 'Well, he saved my life, I suppose,' Emma said, scrupulously fair.

Ami spilled a bit of coffee. 'You didn't tell me that in your postcards,' she accused.

Emma smiled. 'It isn't the kind of thing you write in postcards, is it? "By the way, I got trapped in a bushfire and jumped through it with MCP. Wish you were here."'

'Jumped *through* it?'

She sketched in the situation lightly. The fire, the confusion, the injured wallaby escaping.

'You were chasing a wallaby,' Ami repeated.

'I know, it was a crazy thing to do,' Emma admitted. 'But I'd killed that kangaroo on the road, so I had to.'

'Ah. Of course,' Ami said, grappling with this chain of cause and effect.

'Mackenzie came looking for me, the two fire fronts raced in together and we could have been roasted alive.' Emma looked off into space. She'd dreamed about it several times—the surrounding flames—but in the dreams Mackenzie hadn't come. 'I wonder if his hair will grow back.'

'His hair got burned?'

'He gave his helmet to me. Sprayed me with water and kind of—went sideways to shelter me from the worst.' She'd only realised that, later. 'And he carried the wallaby too, tucked down his overalls.'

'What's his first name?'

'Matt.' Emma swallowed, remembering the only time she'd used his first name. 'Almost everyone calls him "Boss". I didn't, of course.'

'My intuition——'

'But his *wife* probably will. If she doesn't call him Daddy.' It was so bitchy, so unworthy of her that she flushed. 'The wedding could be any time soon.'

'Is there—anything you want to talk about, Emma?' her friend prompted, eyes alight with curiosity.

'That knife-wound you mentioned——'

Ami sighed. 'All right. I know when to stop being nosy.'

'Intuition?' Emma said, grinning.

A month passed. Hot November was followed by the hottest December for decades. But red-suited Santas sweated it out in every suburban shopping centre and swimming togs and bikinis were displayed through windows frosted with artificial snow, scattered with pretend snowflakes. Illusions of a northern hemisphere Christmas in a large Pacific Island. Emma made a flying visit to her parents in Melbourne for Christmas, where the weather turned cool enough to make the artificial snow less laughable.

She repainted her bedroom and started an aerobics class, planted marigolds. Good rain had fallen out west and the drought had officially broken. Now Catastrophe really would celebrate. A time for parades and parties. Weddings. Everything back to normal. The townspeople probably hadn't given any of them a second thought. Mackenzie, she meant. Did he think of her at all? Mackenzie would very likely forget her name. She wouldn't forget his, though. Who could forget a man who didn't have to have his own name up in lights?

On New Year's Eve she read an engagement notice in the *Sydney Morning Herald*. Elisa Jane Crawford to Matthew Bryce Mackenzie. And on the same day, while she was run ragged with the preparations for a New Year's Eve concert at the theatre, Steve Mackenzie turned up.

Her heart skipped a beat when she saw him. She wasn't aware that she had glanced beyond him until Steve said drily, 'I'm alone. Big brother isn't with me.'

She wondered how often people saw Steve as a sign of his brother's possible presence. Mackenzie just couldn't help casting his shadow over his younger brother.

'Could you give me a job, Emma?' he asked. 'Just for a while, until I get on my feet. I've left for good this time.'

'Is it the engagement that's prompted this?'

He lifted his shoulders. 'In a way. Now that Matt's getting married, there's no chance of him leaving to give me a chance to run things. So—time for me to make a move, do my own thing.'

'Was there *ever* any chance of Mackenzie leaving Falkner's?' she asked.

'He used to talk about it—*one day* when I was sensible enough to run the place. But Matt got to like being the Boss. He'll never give it up now.'

She hired him in the end, against her better judgement. But she owed Steve a favour and she liked him and she was short-handed. 'But the only thing you're allowed to do in this theatre until you've joined the union is make my coffee, OK?' But as the new year came in, Emma felt that odd sensation of unfinished business from the old one, and she wondered if it was an omen that a little bit of Catastrophe had come to town just when she could have started the new year with a clean sweep.

Three months later it seemed a good omen, for Steve had settled in well at the theatre, and was a valued companion. He was uncomplicated fun and Emma realised how little of that she'd had in the past few years of hard work. When he had trouble finding lodgings he could afford, Emma rented him her downstairs 'granny flat'. When Mackenzie found out, she thought, he would think the worst. But she didn't dwell on what Mackenzie might think, especially as April approached and Mackenzie showed no interest in the fact that his brother was working for Emma.

'What did Mack—your brother say when you told him you were working here?' she asked once.

Steve shot her an odd look and shrugged. 'Nothing.'

Emma didn't ask again. It was all too tempting to say his name, find out little things about him. The first week in April, another bit of Catastrophe came to town. One cool, windy night, Emma answered her door expecting it to be Steve come to borrow milk or bread, and found instead a girl with glossy brown hair

and a large suitcase. 'Libby?' She couldn't help herself.
Her eyes darted beyond the girl, seeking the biggest
bit of Catastrophe. She passed a hand over her eyes
and suppressed a giggle. As if the prospective bride
and groom would come calling on her!

'I hope you're going to ask me in,' Libby said. She
had her head up and looked an arrogant, spoiled miss,
but Emma heard the tremor in her voice and saw the
sheen in her eyes. She gestured the girl in and Libby
lugged in her case, talking non-stop in a brittle manner.
'I left in a rush and forgot my credit cards,' she said.
'And you're just dross without a credit card. Dad's got
accounts at several hotels but he will have alerted
them.'

'*Alerted*?' Emma said uneasily.

'I suppose it's a bit of a cheek coming here, considering you and Matt——' She gave a flick of one hand
and its eloquence stung colour into Emma's face. 'The
thing is, I have to get away on my own, to think. Just
for a week. That's not much to ask, is it?' she
demanded.

'But—isn't your wedding in one week?' Emma said
stiffly.

'That's just it!' Libby burst out.

Pre-wedding nerves. Did that mean she wouldn't
marry Mackenzie after all? The foolish skip of Emma's
heartbeat annoyed her. Of course she would. Most
women were nervous before the wedding, she knew
from experience, but few cancelled because of it. For a
young country-bred woman in the social backwater of
Catastrophe, Mackenzie was a glittering prize. Emma
did two brisk turns around the room. And Mackenzie's
jittery bride had come to *her*! It was absurd. Emma felt
depressed and ancient.

'If I could stay here just one night—and if you could
just help me find a—a hostel or someplace cheap.'
Libby plucked at the fabric of the divan with her left

hand. A large diamond and sapphire ring glittered on her third finger. 'I've got friends in Sydney but none of them could stand up to—to Dad—or Matt if they come looking for me, and I'd have to go back.' She sank on to the divan and looked warily at Emma. 'You're the only person I know in Sydney who wouldn't cave in the moment they put the pressure on.'

Emma found it a dubious distinction. She had a vision of herself, Boadicea-like, staunchly defending Libby's right to privacy from a furious, determined Mackenzie. She shook her head. No way did she want to see him again. Resentfully she studied the younger woman. Was Libby totally selfish and insensitive, to bring this particular problem and lay it at her feet?

'I know you don't like me,' Libby said, correctly reading Emma's expression. 'But you're the kind of person who doesn't have to like someone before you'll help.'

'Am I?' Emma said drily. 'Boadicea and Mother Teresa rolled into one?'

Libby smiled, and it was the quality of the smile that caught at Emma. The girl was distraught but putting on a brave face. And she was right, of course. Whether Emma liked her or not, she could not in all conscience turn a young woman out on to the streets of Sydney at this time of night. 'I hope you've at least left a note,' Emma said. 'You don't want people worried sick over you. Or do you?'

Libby sat up very straight and pale at that. 'They know why I've gone away, just not where. And I feel guilty enough, already, especially when Dad——' Libby looked as if she might cry, but conquered the urge. 'But I just can't *think* when I'm back there. They have everything organised and they're so—*confident* that they're right, and when I'm with them it's too easy to be swept along with their opinions. They want to look after me because they care about me and if I disagree I

sound like a real bitch—oh, *you* probably don't have
that problem!'

Emma recalled the way Simon had made her feel
disloyal, unloving if she disagreed with his plans. 'Don't
you love me any more, Emma?' he would say, or, 'I'd
have thought I could rely on *your* support.' Seeing the
brightness in Libby's eyes, she put a box of tissues
close by and discreetly withdrew to make some coffee,
hoping Steve wouldn't come knocking at her door until
she'd got rid of Libby. A Catastrophe reunion on her
doorstep was something she wanted to avoid at all
costs. She phoned Ami and asked if she could manage
a house-guest for a few days. 'She'll definitely be gone
by the end of the week, because she's going back home
to Catastrophe for her wedding, once she's got over
the jitters.'

There was an awed silence. 'The Boss's bride? Emma
what are you *doing*? You've already got his little
brother in your basement!'

'Not under duress!' She laughed. 'Will you do it? I'll
owe you.'

Her friend agreed, as Emma knew she would. But
even after Libby had gone to stay with Ami, where at
least she wouldn't run into her future brother-in-law,
Emma was uneasy at the enmeshing of her life with
these threads from Catastrophe.

Three days went by and there were no stern demands
for the return of a daughter or a wife-to-be. Emma
Spencer would be the last person they would think of,
she decided. By now they would have forgotten all
about her.

But Mackenzie hadn't forgotten her. It was she who
had conveniently forgotten that he had a very good
reason to remember her. A visit from a Detective
Inspector Wilson reminded her. Emma was relaxed
and friendly, accustomed to dealing with the police in

tragic cases of runaways and street kids who sought shelter on the theatre precincts.

'We're liaising with regional police about a series of fires,' he said, wiping her co-operative smile away.

Emma stared at him. 'Fires,' she repeated.

'We hoped you might be able to help us with our enquiries.'

Wasn't that what they always said to suspects? The blood rushed from Emma's face.

'If you could take a look at these——' He spread out several photographs—amateur shots, obviously from different cameras, taken backstage at several different venues on their tour.

'That's my crew and me, drinking tea with local townspeople after a show. What has this to do with fires, Inspector?'

He gave a non-committal smile, pointed to several figures one after another and she supplied names as she remembered them. 'That's Bernie with Alison. Alison again with the mayor, or someone. Wayne Sweet, our devoted fan. You can't see him in this one; his face is hidden by the flowers he's carrying. Pink carnations,' she added, looking at him with a touch of temper. 'I can give you much more detail if I know just how much you want.'

'Flowers for you, Ms Spencer?' he said, conversationally, taking back the snaps.

'Yes, unfortunately.'

A faint smile. He dealt out several more photos, like a croupier. 'I thought ladies liked getting flowers. I thought actresses expected it.'

She pulled down her mouth at the unconscious distinction between 'lady' and 'actress'. She was reminded of Mackenzie's sarcastic comments on the same subject. 'Well this lady didn't want flowers from him, Inspector—he started out harmlessly enough with a bunch of violets but ended up a prize nuisance with

massive bouquets of carnations.' She pointed to a
photo. 'That's Reg. Reg again. Look, *what* is this
about? Why am I being questioned in connection with
this matter?'

But of course, she knew. I haven't told anyone else.
This is just between you and me, Mackenzie had said.
The blood rushed to her face. She was hurt, angry,
astonished that he had done this. Her hands trembled
slightly and the officer looked keenly at her. Emma
almost laughed. She probably looked guilty.

'Mackenzie put you on to this line of questioning,
didn't he?' she said, gritting her teeth. 'Matt Mackenzie
and his neat little chart with red stickers and his neat
little half-baked theory.'

A moment of surprise disturbed his bland civil
servant mask and Emma knew it was true. Her colour
rode high as she went through the formalities of seeing
the policeman out. When he'd gone she stood by her
door awhile, then slammed it.

'You swine, Mackenzie!' she muttered. After several
fruitless minutes at her desk, she made two phone calls,
one to Falkner's Place and one to the town councillor's
office in Catastrophe. There was no answer from
either. Mackenzie was out of bounds again. Emma
banged the receiver down. 'If I just knew where you
were, *Boss* Mackenzie——' she muttered, rehearsing
the stinging words she would say to him.

She found out exactly where he was later that
evening. But as usual he saw her first. It was after
eleven, the second successful performance of the South
American Folk Troupe was over but little outbreaks
from pan pipes and Spanish guitars could be heard as
the musicians ironed out some kinks in the dressing-
rooms. Two dancers argued hotly over the rumours of
a political coup back home. The empty theatre echoed
with the sounds of its other life as the performers
prepared to leave and cleaners arrived to perform

without applause. Emma was on the catwalk with Steve, high above the stage, checking a faulty light. There was very little room and she leaned her elbow on Steve's shoulder to peer at the section he pointed out.

'All right. Get it down and we'll replace it,' she was saying when they heard footsteps below. Mackenzie stood on the stage, planted squarely, looking up. Her heart gave a few hefty thuds. He had his hands in his jeans pockets, thumbs hooked on the outside, a leather jacket pushed back. She stared down at him, taking a fierce satisfaction from her high vantage point. Mackenzie looked grimly from his brother to Emma.

'Are you going to come down, or will I come up?' he said, brusquely and Emma wondered if he meant both of them, and if not, which of them. The resonance of his voice held, right up here to the ceiling.

'Three's a crowd,' Steve quipped, and Emma knew he was masking a certain nervousness at facing his brother. That made two of them, she thought. Mackenzie positively simmered. He reverted to his arrogant hands-on-the-hips stance and narrowed his eyes. He looked almost Shakespearian, she thought, trying to decide what powerful feeling was putting the glitter in his eyes. Rage, jealousy, vengeance?

'We're busy, Mackenzie,' she said, taking pleasure in making him wait. 'Please take a seat.' With a certain irony she indicated the auditorium full of them. Mackenzie folded his arms across his chest and ignored the offer.

She made him wait a few minutes then they climbed down the ladder onto the stage.

'You might have let me know you were safe,' Mackenzie said to his brother. With the faintest shift of his gaze to Emma, he added sardonically, 'I presume you *are* safe.'

Emma itched to hit him. The innuendo went over Steve's head.

'Come to invite me to be best man at your wedding, Matt?' he asked, folding his arms and lowering his head in unconscious imitation of his brother.

Mackenzie looked up beneath frowning brows. His rock-solid confidence must have taken a blow when his fiancée ran away. Emma felt a fleeting sympathy for him as Steve unwittingly persisted with the subject of weddings. 'That was a joke, Matt. *Me* as *your* best man!' he said with a self-deprecatory smile.

'I didn't even know you were here, Steve. How could I?' Mackenzie said harshly. 'I came to see——'

He looked at Emma but left it at that, as if he couldn't bring himself to say the name. 'Emma,' she said, helpfully. 'Emma Spencer. Seen any good fires lately, Mackenzie?' It came out savagely, more savagely than she'd meant and the tiny catch in her voice seemed magnified by the stage acoustics. Vacuum cleaners droned and a tattoo sounded as one of the cleaning staff flipped back a row of seats.

To his brother, Mackenzie said, 'Are you working here, then or are you just—socialising?'

'Emma hired me. She's a better boss than you, Matt. You could take lessons from her.'

'I guess that means she lets you do what you like,' Mackenzie drawled. There were pale patches beside his mouth. 'You always preferred to be indulged—and with your looks you can usually find a woman to indulge you.'

Emma caught in her breath at this double-barrelled insult. Steve paled but said hotly, 'And you want to know why she's a better boss? Because she asks my opinion and she's happy to let me make a decision now and then! Because she doesn't have to be the puppet-master pulling all the strings! I can *talk* to her—damned if I can talk to you!'

Mackenzie flinched. A fine film of sweat glistened on his forehead. 'Miss Spencer seems to have been a great influence on you. Just how far does that influence extend?'

There was a malicious gleam in Steve's eyes. 'I live in her house—is that what you want to know?'

Mackenzie's head went back like a boxer evading a blow. Emma stepped between the brothers like a referee. 'That—is—*enough*!' she yelled.

Her voice carried to the back row, over the drone of vacuum cleaners and the operators looked up curiously. Emma glowered at the two men.

'This is *my* theatre. If you want to prove what tough men you are, go and brawl in the alley out the back! And please don't use *me* to score points off each other!' She whirled on Mackenzie, eyes blazing. 'It's none of your business what my precise relationship with your brother is, but I'll tell you anyway. I am his boss and I am his landlady and, I hope, his friend. You should develop a little faith in your brother. It would be a pity if you went through life a misogynist *and* a cynic!'

At Steve's snort of laughter, she turned on him. 'What are *you* laughing at? All along I assumed you'd had the decency to let your only brother know what you were doing! I can't believe you could be so heartless—would it have hurt you to send a postcard so that he could stop worrying and sleep nights? He might have a funny way of showing it but he cares about you—'

'I don't need you to intercede for me,' Mackenzie ground out.

'No? Got all your relationships under control, have you? Your younger brother alienated, your bride with the jitters—' Emma bit her lip, cursing herself for the giveaway.

There was a passionate little bout of strumming from a guitar down below in the dressing-rooms. Mackenzie

grabbed her arm, hauled her in. 'You've seen her!' he
snarled, staring into her eyes. Emma felt the ebb and
flow of his breath on her face. There was a faint whisky
smell on it. 'Well, well, this is a regular lost-and-found
department—and I thought it was a long shot, coming
here.' He gave Emma a shake. 'Where is she?'

'You fiancée is—perfectly safe. She says she wants
some time to think.'

'Think about what?'

'You're marrying her next week,' Emma hissed.
'Don't you have any clues?'

Mackenzie eyed her grimly. 'Tell me where she is.'

'She asked me not to do that.'

He looked shaken, hurt, and Emma was moved to
say, more soothingly, 'She just wants some time to
herself.'

'Don't patronise me by feeling sorry for me,' he said
through gritted teeth.

'Sorry for *you*!' She wrenched her arm from his grasp
and gave an artificial laugh that coursed merrily to the
back rows. 'It's Libby I feel sorry for. Straight from a
boss man father to a boss man husband. All she's
asking is one week to herself and as far as I am
concerned, that's what she'll get.'

'I'll find out,' he said harshly. 'Her father won't rest
until she goes back home. He's—not in good health.'

'She left him a note telling him what she was doing
and why.'

'If she loved him she wouldn't worry him like this.'

'If he loved her, he would accept her right to be
alone.'

And so would you, she said silently, conveying the
opinion with a level look. Mackenzie took a few paces
down left, clenching and unclenching his fists. He let
loose with a short, sharp expletive. The night cleaners
were now watching the stage as they worked, following

the free entertainment, straining to hear over the sound of the machines.

'*Why*?' Mackenzie bellowed at the ceiling, his arms spread, his head tipped back. The question asked by humans from the beginning of time. He rammed his hand through his hair. 'What can I do? I don't *know* what to do!' It was a roar of frustration, of powerlessness, but even as he made the admission his hands went down to his hips and he glared at Emma. 'Everything was all right until the circus came to town. Now suddenly, everyone is making dramatic gestures. Running away from——' He stopped suddenly as if about to bite down on a cyanide capsule. One big hand swept in an arc, indicating the theatre. 'Everyone ends up at *your* door!'

All the vacuum cleaners switched off. 'Well, it can't be anything *you're* doing wrong.' Emma said, hands on hips. 'So it must be witchcraft. I put a spell on them.'

'I could almost believe that,' he said, hardly moving his mouth.

'You could believe anything of me! First I was a temptress, putting your little brother in moral danger. Then I was a blabbermouth making trouble with your fiancée, *then* I was a firebug! I hope you have a good lawyer. . .'

'I wish you wouldn't call me his "little brother",' Steve said plaintively.

Neither Emma or Mackenzie heard him. 'If someone told you I usually pop on a balaclava and do a few burglaries on the way home from the theatre at nights, you'd probably believe that too! Watch yourself, Mackenzie. If you don't stop being so suspicious, people might start to think you're afraid of me!'

'Damned right,' he snarled. 'What the hell do you mean about a lawyer?'

'If my reputation or that of the theatre's is damaged in any way because of your suspicious mind, I will take legal action, Mackenzie.' Her voice was low and strong. 'That—I promise you!'

'I'm shaking all over, Lady Macbeth,' he mocked.

Out back, Reg moved a piece of furniture that dragged along the timber floor. The pulleys started and a sky-blue backdrop fell into place. It looked like a hot November sky over Catastrophe.

'Hey, Boss!' Reg called from behind it.

Emma and Mackenzie answered 'Yes,' simultaneously, out of habit.

'He means me,' she said, with immense satisfaction. Two vacuum cleaners switched on in whining applause. The two Mackenzies moved belligerently towards each other as Emma escaped backstage.

All her fine fury at Mackenzie dissipated in the knowledge that she could only hurt herself with it. Now that she'd seen him again she was confused, more desolate than angry. The sense of loss was stunning. Loss of what? she asked herself. It wasn't as if there was anything but chemistry between herself and Mackenzie. And the way her life had gone, the last thing she wanted was anything more than that. Yet this puzzling feeling persisted. As if there was something she had forgotten, or misplaced, and couldn't quite remember what it was, only that it was somewhere, waiting. Emma braced her shoulders to throw off this blue mood. Maybe, she thought prosaically, Mackenzie was like the occasional cup of coffee she misplaced in the course of a busy day. She always felt that odd feeling that she hadn't finished something. But in the end all she ever found under a pile of papers was a cold cup of coffee.

CHAPTER NINE

BOTH Mackenzie and Steve had gone by the time Emma went home. In her driveway she saw Steve's lights on and wondered if his brother was there with him. Upstairs, she paced about, considering and rejecting various landlady-like excuses for knocking at his door, to find out. In her bed, she held her breath, trying to pick up the sound of voices. One voice, anyway. Disgusted with herself, she turned to the ever-present pile of manuscripts beside her bed. As if by evil design, the next item for her attention was Sara Hardy's play. Grimly, she turned to page one, wondering if by any chance something good might yet come out of Catastrophe.

The first thing Emma did in the morning was to phone Ami.

'You are a friend, after all, and I wouldn't want you to be confronted by Mackenzie without warning. How's Libby?'

'She's helping me at the shop,' Ami said. 'If you want my opinion, I don't think she's going to marry him.'

Emma felt a lurching sensation in her stomach. 'Of course she will,' she said, flatly. 'Though the way I feel at the moment nothing would give me greater pleasure than to see him jilted at the altar.'

'What a terrible thing to say about a man who saved your life.'

Emma felt a pang of remorse. Her debt to Mackenzie far outweighed any treacherous behaviour on his part. She tried to remember that later, when she went outside to water her garden before dressing for the office. Parked in the street was a battered utility truck, faded red, dusty, mud-splashed. Even in Sydney it was one of a kind. And it hadn't been there when she came back from her aerobics class earlier. The jet of water crushed a clump of marigolds as she stared at the truck. Its front fender was crumpled, the headlight smashed. Emma's heart gave a few thuds in recognition of her need for strength as she looked around for the driver. He was leaning against the downstairs door, arms crossed, watching her. Again that spasm of irritation that he always saw her first. Except that one time. Emma met his gaze through the fountain of water, disorientated enough to let herself dwell on the pleasure of watching him that night while he remained unaware—bare legged, his big body somehow more vulnerable when he wasn't commanding it so fiercely.

Now, he raised a hand and turned away as the water spray reached him. She turned the hose off and tossed it down, wishing she were already dressed for work. When she'd changed from her gym gear she'd put on a cheesecloth wrap-over long skirt and an old, stretched sweater that advertised the absence of a bra and slipped continually sideways over one shoulder. She yanked it back into place and went over to him.

Mackenzie's eyes moved, but that was all. He stayed there, shouldered into the wall, his body on an incline, arms crossed. A pair of sunglasses were shoved into the pocket of his crumpled shirt. The bags under his eyes were more noticeable this morning and he looked pale in the sunlight. The singed patch of hair had grown again, straight and spiky, except for one small spot on the hairline where the hair had regrown into a whorl. He was at least a day overdue for a shave and looked as if he hadn't slept in days. Searching, she supposed, for Libby.

'You look awful,' she said sharply, dragging her eyes away from him the way someone starving might drag their eyes from a feast. She almost laughed. A feast of Mackenzie. Who had a stomach strong enough?

'You look great.' His eyes extended the compliment, warmed it. After the way he'd looked at her last night it came as a shock. Emma tried to stem the pleasure she felt. He had no right to look at her like this. She had no right to like it.

'Steve's already left, so it's no good knocking on his door.'

'Steve has his own door?'

'His own door, his own life, his own bed,' she snapped. Tapping the door, she added, 'This is a self-contained flat. I've let it out for years. The rent helps pay off my mortgage. My tenant happened to vacate it when Steve was looking for a place, so——' She shrugged, annoyed to have explained so much. 'A business arrangement.' She felt a spasm of irritation at the complacency this information seemed to generate.

'Where is *your* door?'

'You think I'm going to invite you in, Mackenzie?' Her heart was going like a steam hammer. There was a look in his eyes she couldn't pin down. A sudden sultriness on this cool, autumn morning. Deliberately she conjured up a picture of Libby, dressed in lace, veiled in white. Beside Libby, she put Mackenzie in a dove-grey suit and a burgundy ascot. Catastrophe's wedding of the year. We are gathered together. . .

'I hoped you would. I've come to call in a favour.'

Emma stiffened. She owed Mackenzie a favour. The biggest of them all. He would ask her to break a promise to Libby because he'd saved her life. 'I see.'

'I could have gone somewhere else——'

'But you figured I owed you more than anyone else,' she said distastefully. Well, at least Libby had had a couple of days to herself before discovery, she thought.

'You haven't forgotten already?'

'No.' Emma looked down her nose at him, a difficult

task even when he had reduced his height by slouching. 'I suppose I can hardly refuse you.'

'Good.' He straightened and wearily rotated his shoulders. 'Lead me to it.'

'To what?'

'Your shower.'

It took her a few moments to work it out. In spite of herself, she smiled. 'That's the favour? You want to use my shower, Mackenzie? Is that all?'

He smiled back. 'And a towel. Please.'

She laughed. 'I thought you were going to demand I tell where Libby is to repay you for getting me through the fire.'

Mackenzie touched the back of his hand to her cheek. It was so gentle, so unexpected that she felt a weakness in her knees. It took every ounce of will-power to resist the urge to incline her head towards his touch, to prolong it. She brought up the wedding picture in her mind, tossed a little confetti over Mackenzie's broad shoulders. I now pronounce you boss and wife. . .

'I told you, getting you through the fire was just part of my job. Letting you use my shower. . .now that was a sacrifice and deserves to be repaid.'

'Sacrifice? I didn't use much water,' she protested.

'I sacrificed my peace of mind,' he said gravely. What was it about him that was different? A teasing quality—a lack of tension, something. He went to his truck to fetch a bag and she followed. As he opened the door with his left hand she saw that he was favouring his right which was wrapped in a blood-stained handkerchief.

'You've hurt yourself.'

Ruefully he glanced at it. 'A slight accident during the night. I drove into a park fence.'

Emma looked at the crumpled front of the truck then at his hand. 'Damn it, Mackenzie! It's no wonder, if you've been on the road non-stop for the last two days. What were you doing *driving* all the way from Catastrophe in your state of mind? Why didn't you fly?'

And even as she asked the question she knew the answer by the way he averted his eyes. Because by driving he could pass through all those towns, searching the parking strips for a motorbike. Emma felt an overwhelming empathy with him. How lonely a trip it must have been, worrying about Libby, looking for his missing brother along the way.

'Reading my mind again, Emma?' he said drily, looking at her face and reading hers.

It was altogether too intimate. She gave herself a shake.

'And you certainly shouldn't have been driving last night—you'd been drinking—I could smell it on your breath. You're lucky you didn't injure yourself seriously.' When he eyed her quizzically at this wifely outburst of concern, she turned to lead the way to her own front door and added, more for her own benefit than anything, 'I'm sure Libby would prefer her groom without bandages and plaster casts.'

'Libby would prefer no groom at all,' he said.

Emma stopped so suddenly that Mackenzie walked into her. She looked over her shoulder at him. 'What?'

'She changed her mind about getting married. I've been jilted, Emma,' he said with a hangdog expression.

Her heartbeat discovered a reggae rhythm. No wedding. Libby not to be a bride dressed in lace, veiled in white. Mackenzie not to be a groom. No wedding bells. No confetti. Mackenzie, free. The wedding photo was suddenly a blank, waiting to be filled. One part of her exulted, another curled up in apprehension. Straight-backed, she walked up the steps and opened her front door to Mackenzie. 'I'm sorry it didn't work out,' she said seriously. 'It must be very distressing to—everyone when a wedding is cancelled. Libby's father, Joyce——'

'Joyce will break open the champagne when she finds out,' he said drily. 'She's been waging a campaign against it ever since she spilled the beans about me and you together on my office divan.'

'Oh, well. At least you know it wasn't me who blabbed,' she said lamely. She simply couldn't think of anything else to say on the subject. She led Mackenzie to the bathroom, hurrying him past her shelved collections in the living-room when he would have lingered. She took a towel from her linen closet. 'When you've showered, I'll tape something over your hand,' she said. He stared at her frankly as she walked down the hall towards him, the way a child stared at something or someone before he learned that such directness was not allowed to adults. When she offered him the towel, he didn't take it. He looked, she thought a little punch-drunk. 'Were you hit on the head in this accident?' He didn't answer, just went on looking at her in a mute way as if he had lost the art of language. 'Mackenzie?'

'Um—bump on the head. Nothing much,' he mumbled.

It was so unlike him that she leaned in close to check his pupils. They seemed normal. So green, his eyes. So unusually vulnerable. 'I don't know what to do. . .' Some of Mackenzie's arrogance had crumbled during his journey. There was uncertainty in him and something else it was hard to pin down. She couldn't stop looking into his eyes. To break the thrall she thrust the towel at him and said, briskly and belatedly. 'Park fence? What were you doing at a park during the night? You surely didn't think you'd find Libby on a park bench?' Her eyes narrowed. 'Where did you sleep last night?'

'Beside the park, in the truck. It's every bit as uncomfortable as your van must have been.'

He went into the bathroom and unwrapped his hurt hand. 'I left it a bit late to book into a hotel—and I was too tired to look for one anyway. I had to check out all Libby's schoolfriends after I left the theatre, you see——' He sent her a dour look. 'You could have saved me a terrible night, Emma.'

Her eyes widened. It struck her that he must have found out about Libby's decision some time between last night and this morning. 'You *found* her, didn't you?'

Mackenzie shrugged his big shoulders out of the leather jacket. 'This morning. I remembered you talking about your friend Ami Winter-something. When I found an Ami Winterburn in the phone book listed as 'theatrical supplier', I figured it was worth following up. I found Libby in your friend's shop, with a black eye and bruises on her arm,' he said reflectively.

Emma grinned. 'Ami does the best bruises in town.'

He looked rueful and Emma guessed he must have cut up rough a bit until he realised Libby's injuries were an illusion. He unbuttoned his shirt absently, looking at her.

'She is some lady. Are all your friends as formidable as you?'

She laughed softly. Ami wouldn't have allowed even Mackenzie to cut up rough unchallenged. 'As I said, Ami and I are more like sisters.' Simon, she remembered suddenly, had not appreciated Ami's robust personality and for nearly two years she had seen little of her friend because Simon made it so very difficult.

There was a shimmer of muscle as Mackenzie pulled his shirt off over his head. His chest hair hadn't grown back, she noted. There was a mere stubble over one side of his chest, wiry curls where the hair had not been burned. The scar over his ribs was a faint pink line. He tossed the shirt down and met her gaze with the faint smile of a man who knew he was being looked at and assumed the opinion was favourable. There was plenty of male arrogance left intact, she decided.

'You remembered Ami's name?' she said. 'I'm sure I only mentioned her in passing.'

'Are you impressed?' he asked. He raised his hands to massage his neck tiredly and she wondered if he meant his memory or his muscles.

She flicked a look over all the rippling motion going on in deltoids and biceps and very nice pectorals and said, 'Not especially.' But she was. To remember a name said once, he had to have listened. And a man who genuinely listened was a rarity. Simon always gave a very good imitation, which had passed scrutiny until she woke up one day without stars in her eyes and a cigarette lighter to light up cigarettes she no longer smoked.

Emma left, closing the door with a decided snap before Mackenzie started holding his breath to make himself even more impressive. She washed up her breakfast things and boiled the kettle, dropped tea-bags in two cups. She owed him that, she supposed, wondering where he would go when he'd had his shower. And all the time pictures played in her head as if she had not left the bathroom but was there, unseen, watching Mackenzie discard his trousers and underclothes to stand naked in her old-fashioned bath.

To start a fire, Mackenzie had told her once, you needed three things. Heat, oxygen, fuel. Which of the three, she wondered, was Mackenzie? She only knew when he wasn't around there were no sparks like this, no small flames starting. She laid the palms of her hands to her face, startled by the heat of her skin. Damn Libby, she thought. She had hated the idea of her marrying him, but now that she wasn't she had to deal with this. Which was worse? She wondered if he was wearing the underpants with parasols on them?

'For heaven's sake!' she muttered.

In the circumstances, she rather regretted offering to fix his hand. When she knocked at the door after the shower had stopped, and Mackenzie opened it, her misgivings multiplied. Mackenzie, seen mistily through steam, a towel wrapped around his waist, hair wet, jaw still bearing the traces of shaving cream. He rinsed a razor out beneath running water and, seeing her interest in the ritual, said. 'I've never taken to electric shavers. I'm an old-fashioned man.'

'Yes, you told me,' she said. 'Sit down on the bath-bench and I'll stick a plaster over the scratch on your hand.'

It was more than a scratch. The gash was almost deep enough for stitches. Bending to the job, with some antiseptic spray, she said, 'This will sting.'

Mackenzie looked up at her and smiled and it was a languid, sensual affair that sent little warning rushes along her spine. 'It stung last time.'

'When?' she said, thrown by him in this mood, whatever the mood was. The steam had drifted away but the bathroom remained as sultry as a northern rainforest.

'Last time you tended my wounds.'

The timbre of his voice was enhanced by the bathroom acoustics. Like trickles of warm water on her skin. Emma turned away to the cabinet for some plasters. 'Hardly wounds, would you say?' Why do I keep asking questions, she despaired. Ask him questions and he answers in that voice. 'Keep still,' she said sharply to forestall any answer.

She applied a plaster, then crossed it with another.

'I didn't intend to go to your theatre last night,' he said. 'I told myself it was the flimsiest of excuses to see you again, to go there asking about Libby. Ironic.'

Emma didn't answer. The flimsiest of excuses to see you again. . . It made her heartbeat erratic again, the thought that he had wanted to see her. But he seemed

to think of it as a kind of failure—he had valiantly tried
to resist seeing the devil-woman again, but had failed.

'There,' she said. As she straightened, she saw a
patch of dark red in his hair and leaned over him to
investigate. Gently she prodded the swelling and he
groaned. 'You've broken the skin.' She reached for the
antiseptic spray and he groaned again. 'It might sting a
bit, that's all,' she said surprised at this uncharacteristic
behaviour. 'Don't be such a wimp. Think of something
else.'

'I am thinking of something else,' he said in a muffled
voice so odd that she looked down. His head was level
with her chest and Emma felt the huff of his breath
through the sweater. Her breasts, unconfined by a bra,
swayed with the small backward movement of her
body. The sweater clung to their contours and the clear
shape of her nipples. Mackenzie had a bemused
expression on his face. He raised his eyes to her and
said, gravely, 'I'm thinking of the theory of perpetual
motion.'

'Oh, grow up, Mackenzie,' she said, flushing, and
administered a cold blast of antiseptic to his head. She
stepped back smartly to snap the lid on the spray can.

'Have dinner with me tonight, Emma,' he said.

Everything was crumbling around her. The defences
she'd built up had relied too heavily on Libby as a
foundation. She didn't want to get involved, not with a
man who wanted to boss everything and everyone. If
she said yes to dinner, what then? There was no Libby
to limit what might happen. No guilt for Mackenzie to
hold him back. No safety net for her. Her pulses
drummed away, stimulated by the notion of Mackenzie
with all stops off. She shoved the spray in the cabinet
and fumbled it, catching the can as it fell out again.

'The grieving bridegroom,' she said caustically. 'One
day you're about to say "I do" and the next day it's all
off and you're inviting another woman to dinner!'

Mackenzie stood, the bemused expression gone. In its place was a more recognisable, flinty look. 'It's not like that, and you know it.'

'I know that I keep clear of men who think of women as interchangeable conveniences,' she said virtuously.

'What?' he said on a note of incredulity. '*You*—interchangeable? Convenient? Ha!' He took up his boss man pose, hands low on his hips. It should have lost something in the translation considering he was wearing only a pale apricot towel. Emma's anger grew, fuelled by the look of him, standing there crowding her out of her own bathroom, with the line of his bare shoulders like the contours of a rugged mountain range testimony to his physical strength—the burn scars a reminder that he had great mental strength to match his muscles. Damn the man!

'You should show a little moral fortitude, Mackenzie,' she sniped, picking up his discarded clothes with a disapproving air. 'At least have the decency to *pretend* you're cut up about being jilted before you start painting the town red!'

'It was a dinner invitation. I wasn't suggesting that we leap into bed together,' he drawled. 'Not immediately.'

Emma flushed. Mackenzie showed his teeth in a sardonic smile. Driven, she shoved his clothes at him. One item clung to her arm and she snatched it off, tossed it with the others. It was, she noticed, a pair of underpants patterned with parasols.

'I—care about Libby, but I've been aware for some time that she and I weren't right for each other,' he said flatly. 'Since last November.' He paused to let that sink in. Emma remembered the hottest November for sixty years and felt a panicky sense of fate closing in on her. 'But I wasn't in a position to just run out on a commitment. It hasn't come as a shock to me that Libby's changed her mind. I could have wished for

better circumstances but it's a bloody relief,'
Mackenzie said.

'So, having warned me off when you were technically
already taken, you're now putting yourself back in
circulation, is that it?' she enquired sweetly. 'Has it
occurred to you that *I* might have lost interest over the
last five months?'

She turned away to straighten diligently all the items
around the vanity basin. Toothbrush, toothpaste,
soap. . . Mackenzie loomed up behind her, reflected in
the mirror, with the tangle of large-leafed philodendrons behind him. He placed his bundle of clothes on
the counter top with a certain deliberation that made
Emma nervous. He stretched an arm either side of her,
resting his hands on the counter, and she felt the
steamy warmth emanating from him.

'Mackenzie——' she said. 'Don't.'

'Don't what?' He watched her in the mirror, his eyes
suddenly sleepy looking. He leaned in closer, inhaling
audibly.

'Don't—whatever it is you're thinking about——' she
said inanely.

'Ah, you must mean this,' he muttered and, keeping
his eyes on her face in the mirror, bent and put his
mouth to the bare skin of her shoulder exposed by the
side-slipping sweater, as if he'd marked out the spot in
advance. Emma's eyes closed involuntarily, her lips
parted on a sigh. 'Or maybe this,' he said warmly in
her ear, and dizzily she watched Mackenzie's big hands
slide around her midriff and edge upwards. Just in time
she forestalled him and put up her hands to cover her
breasts. Mackenzie simply slid his own hands over hers
and pressed and fondled so that his caresses were
relayed to her through her own hands. Emma gasped
and pulled her arms away and he smiled wickedly at
her in the mirror and rubbed his palms over her
generous contours. It was eroticism such as she'd never

experienced—the sight of Mackenzie's hands moving on her, the sensation of his near-naked body behind her, the tingle in her hands that he had moulded to her own body. Emma could not avoid the evidence of her own arousal in her heavy-lidded eyes, her nipples hardening into prominence as Mackenzie delicately buffed at them with the backs of his fingers. His hands came up to her shoulders. He kissed her exposed shoulder once more and adjusted the wanton neckline.

'And it did occur to me that you might have lost interest over the past months,' he went on, watching her like a hawk. 'But now that I've seen you again——' He put some emphasis on that 'seen' and smiled at her dazed, shocked face in the mirror. 'And now that you've seen yourself. . .' he said softly, inviting her to check the evidence.

Scarlet, Emma pushed him aside and strode off to her bedroom, resisting the urge to run once she realised Mackenzie was following her. A niggle of panic got her, quickening her steps. The long, wrap-over skirt flared out behind her, exposing her legs to the cool air. Her hair flew out in the slipstream. Behind her Mackenzie groaned again.

She turned to close the door but Mackenzie was an immoveable force planted in the doorway. He looked past her at the bed, with a yearning expression that he transferred to her without any alteration.

'Don't even think about it,' she snapped.

'But I do. Too often. Ever get the feeling, Emma, that there is unfinished business between us?' His voice was huskily low, his eyes on the brass bed with its hand-crocheted spread and lace half-curtains and apricot taffeta cushions. He passed a hand over his eyes as if to prolong some inner vision. 'For a new-fashioned woman, you have old-fashioned tastes in bedrooms.'

She gave him an old-fashioned look then opened her wardrobe and took out two hangers of clothes for

work, hanging them on the doorknob. She saw her
gold lighter on the dressing-table and swiped it to drop
in her pocket. Emma stared at the lucky talisman a
moment, letting it do what it had always done for her.
Remember Simon? Remember how besotted you
became with him, how you gave up living your own life
to live his? Simon was a pussycat compared to
Mackenzie. And she had never felt quite like this about
Simon. She broke out in a light sweat. She'd lived with
Simon, been his wife, been his lover, but now she knew
she was more involved emotionally with Mackenzie
than she could ever have been with Simon. Emma
stared at the inscription on the lighter and confronted
an idea she'd been trying to avoid. Not love. She
couldn't possibly love a man she'd only known for a
few days. A man who wanted her but against his will.
A man who saw her as some kind of temptation he had
to resist. Until now. Now that he was no longer honour-
bound he probably wanted to get her out of his system.
Tidy up his unruly emotions, get everything under
control again. She *wouldn't* fall in love with a man like
that. Perversely, she tossed the lighter and said, 'What
a pity you didn't have this to give the police as Exhibit
A.'

Mackenzie's eyes narrowed. 'What are you talking
about?'

'Did you just give them my name or did you hand
over your dinky little chart and a printout of our tour
itinerary and let them make the connection
themselves?'

He got up, abruptly very tense, very wary. But not
surprised. 'The police have been to see you?'

'Don't pretend innocence,' she said contemptuously.
'Of course they've been to see me, asking questions
about my people, poking around the theatre. I don't
appreciate it.'

He looked calculating rather than ashamed. 'Have you had any—trouble, Emma?'

'Trouble enough—"helping the police with their enquiries",' she said caustically. 'Would you mind waiting in the living-room? I want to dress for work.'

He was in the living-room when she had finished dressing, still bare-chested and wrapped in the fluffy apricot towel. Her house had taken on a subtly different atmosphere with this big, half-naked male wandering about making himself at home. He was standing by her display shelves, holding a chunk of rose quartz from her rock collection and looked lingeringly at her trousers, high-necked amethyst body-suit and her tightly plaited hair. 'You said you collected things,' he said, putting the quartz down alongside the vermilion-streaked rock she'd picked up that day on his land. 'You didn't say you were a fanatic.' He looked at a group of thunder-eggs, some free-form pottery, a collection of things washed up from the sea. 'All the elements. Earth, water——' He picked up a fire-blackened acacia seed pod, burst open and empty. 'Fire. Are you creating your own little world here, Emma?'

'It's just my hobby,' she said.

'Do you plan to collect anything special in the future?'

'I don't *plan* to collect,' she said. 'That's just the point. It's spontaneous.'

'And do you ever toss any of the old stuff out?'

Emma felt quite defensive. She looked possessively at her crammed shelvs, experienced a pang of anxiety at the idea of tossing any of it out. 'Why should I?'

'You might find yourself short of space eventually.'

'I can always move to a bigger house.'

'You'd give up your house for a collection of rocks and dead leaves but not for a man?' he mocked, reminding her of the litany she'd quoted to him months ago. She wouldn't give up her name, her job or her house for a man, she'd said.

'I might, if I found a man who had more to offer me than rocks and dead leaves do,' she said.

'And what do they offer, Emma?'

'Oh,' she said lightly, 'I talk to them and they never interrupt or tell me I shouldn't worry my pretty little head over something, or say that I'm beautiful when I'm angry instead of taking me seriously. I only have to dust them, never have to wash their socks or cook a special dinner to coax them out of their sulks. They never demand to know where I've been and they never say, "If you loved me, you'd think more of me than your damned work and stay home".' She'd said too much and she could see Mackenzie fitting it together, making a picture of the way it had been for her and Simon, and it was one picture in which she could only look a fool. 'I'm making tea,' she announced, much in the way she might say 'I'm spraying insecticide'.

He followed her to the kitchen. Without comment he viewed the walls, hung with old copper pans and antique spoons and ladles, inspected the display hatch filled to overflowing with crazed blue and white plates. The whites of his eyes showed as he scrutinised the plethora of cooking pots old and new that hung from black ceiling hooks. Emma had a disconcerting sensation that somewhere in her décor there were secrets that Mackenzie was reading. 'Well—what do you think?' she challenged.

He looked at the remains of a chocolate cake under a glass dome. Emma had forgotten about that. His eyes came back to her and they were warm and soft with some knowledge he thought he had of her now. She thought of the way she'd looked in the mirror—unable to hide any damned thing from him and her face grew hot again. 'Do you know that you're beautiful when you're embarrassed?' he said.

She gave a snort and grabbed the kettle as it switched off.

'You collect people too,' he said, watching her pour boiling water on teabags.

'Of course I don't.'

'Your stockman admirer followed you from town to town. Steve. . . Libby. Me. I'm here.'

'You're here looking for the others.'

'Am I?' he took the cup of tea she handed him, raised it. 'You could always read the tea-leaves for clues.'

Emma held out the sugar bowl. She smirked. 'No chance. I made it with teabags.'

The phone rang and she drank her tea while she answered it to deal with a minor hitch in a coming lease package. When she hung up, only Mackenzie's empty teacup was in the living-room and all the chocolate cake was gone. By now, with luck, he would have gone too.

But he hadn't. He lay sprawled on her hand-crocheted bedspread, framed in the scallop-edged lace curtains. Emma took a few steps closer, unable to resist. One muscular arm lay outstretched over a scatter of cushions, the other clasped his bundle of clothes to his side. She should wake him, tell him he couldn't stay here. She touched his shoulder but he was breathing deeply in the sleep of the exhausted. Emma felt a tenderness for him—easier when he was unconscious. She touched her fingertips to his shoulder, let them trail self-indulgently a little way over the rugged mountain-range contours of his outflung arm. He muttered something indistinguishable and turned on to his back. One muscled leg flung itself sideways and the pastel apricot towel came adrift. There were limits to her voyeurism. Emma went.

She got through the day on automatic, apparently fulfilling her obligations satisfactorily, for nobody accused her of daydreaming. The rumoured South American coup had happened overnight and the dressing-rooms had to be diplomatically reorganised to accomodate political affiliations. The translator hid in Emma's office drinking black coffee. Floral tributes arrived backstage ready for final curtain. The orchestra tuned up. Steve went about his work darkly brooding. All he'd said about last night to Emma was, 'I've never heard Matt say that he didn't know what to do.'

'Maybe he thought he had to be a tower of strength when you were seven, and it got to be a habit.'

Steve stared. 'Maybe. I just always assumed he could handle anything. I wonder why Libby ran out on him.' He brightened visibly, let loose a long whistle. 'Matt, jilted. I can't believe it.'

'*I* can't believe you're enjoying your brother's misfortune.'

'Not *enjoying* exactly. Just—glad to find out he can foul up like me. And how come you're so hot in his defence?' Steve gave her a sly, speculative look.

She thrust a lighting plan at him. 'Prove to me you're not just another pretty face and go and check this for me with the electrician, will you? I've got strong premonitions of disaster. If we get the spotlights on the wrong guitar player tonight, it could cause an international incident.'

Steve, she thought, had a long way to go before he had anything like his brother's depth. But she too, wondered why Libby had broken the engagement. A phone call to Ami had left her none the wiser. 'She didn't go into details,' Ami told her. 'Her father came and she thanked me prettily, wiped off one of my better flesh wounds, packed her bag and went off with him. She said she would call you before she went home.'

As it happened, Libby called in person at the theatre, a scant half-hour before the South American troupe was scheduled to start its performance. It was the worst possible time and Emma had a dozen things to do at once, but curiosity got the better of her. She quickly delegated the most pressing jobs and led the way to her office, casting a suspicious look at a distant bunch of pink carnations bobbing along with several dancers. Reminders of the Catastrophe tour were almost a daily occurrence, she thought wearily. But if these carnations were the offering of an unwanted fan, they were headed for the dancers' dressing-room. Emma turned into her office and offered Libby a seat which the girl refused with a tiny shake of her head. She was petite and pretty in pink designer jeans with braces and a pink and grey striped sweater.

'I've broken my engagement to Matt,' she announced.

'Oh.' Emma tried to look as if this was news to her. She tried to look sympathetic, sorrowful, but neither seemed quite right.

'Dad hasn't been well for a long time and I found out, you see—that—well, he's terminally ill. Cancer.'

Emma's sympathy was quite genuine now. 'Libby— I am so sorry.'

The girl's eyes moistened but tears didn't develop. Her chin went up. 'He didn't tell me because. . . I've always been his little girl.' She walked around, looking at the posters on Emma's wall, the autographed photographs of artists. 'He wanted to protect me from all the nasty things of life, I suppose. Matt too. *He* knew Dad only had a year or so to live. Dad confided in him, but not in me.' Her head bowed for a moment as she studied a free-form sculpture dedicated to Emma by a grateful playwright. 'If things had gone the way Dad wanted, I would have been safely married to Matt before I found out. All wrapped up in cotton-wool.'

No wonder Mackenzie had felt committed, Emma thought. Not just to Libby but to his good friend, John

Crawford, a sick man who wanted desperately to see his daughter safely married and in the care of a man he trusted. And what was it Mackenzie had said? 'I waited long enough. It was time I settled down and had a family.'

'They both love me in their way,' Libby said with supreme confidence. 'And I suppose I wanted to please Dad and it was easy to fall for Matt. I mean, I knew eventually I would have to marry *someone* and there's not a great deal of choice around Catastrophe. Matt was the most eligible man around, and the best looking. Except, maybe for Steve. He needs to grow up a bit, but he's a babe.' She rolled her eyes in appreciation of Steve's good looks and Emma gave a cough of laughter.

'What will you do now?'

'Dad was intending to go off to Scotland—you know, a nostalgic return to the place of his ancestors and all that. Except, I'm not sure he was planning to come back. That way I wouldn't have to see him die.' She shook back her glossy hair. 'Well—I'm going to be with him. I know it won't be easy. Dad doesn't want me to see him getting weaker. He wants me to remember him strong and infallible, thinks I'll fall to pieces if he's anything else. Men can be so *stupid*,' she said, her voice wavering a bit. 'That's what I had to think through when I came down here,' she explained. 'And I want to thank you for helping me. Ami is terrific. Oh, Dad—you remember Emma Spencer.'

Her father had come looking for her and stood, countryman's hat in hand, in the doorway of Emmas's office. He said a courteous 'Good evening,' to Emma but he was cool, thinking perhaps of the infamous night on the office divan. He came in to put his arm bracingly around his daughter's shoulders.

'I'm very sorry to hear about—your illness,' Emma said.

He waved that aside. 'I suppose she's told you she

has broken her engagement because she has some scatterbrained scheme to come to Scotland and look after me?' He patted his daughter fondly. 'But I won't hear of it. I still haven't given up hope that she and Matt will make a match of it. He's a man in a million.' He directed another hard look at Emma and she suspected she was being warned that Mackenzie wasn't up for grabs just yet. Taking Libby's elbow, he steered her firmly to the door, saying 'I wonder where he's got to—I want to have a chat with him before we fly home.'

Emma flushed, wondering what he would say if she told him that the man in a million had been asleep naked on her bed only hours ago, framed in lace, like a valentine.

John shook hands with Emma and ushered his daughter into the corridor, still under the impression that he was the boss. Libby and her father were caught up in a sudden influx of musicians carrying guitars and pan pipes. Another large bunch of pink flowers nodded along on the far side of the crowd. So much pink around today, Emma thought as Libby suddenly left her father and came darting back. 'I needn't tell you this, I suppose, but he never kissed me once after you left Catastrophe,' she said, holding Emma's gaze. 'Not properly. Forehead and cheek jobs, you know.' Her chin tilted higher. 'I know you think I'm just a frivolous butterfly, but I would have made him happy if I'd married him.'

Emma gave a strangled laugh. 'Goodbye, butterfly,' she said drily. 'Send me a postcard from Scotland.'

He never kissed me once after you left. . . Emma found the information edifying. She was still turning it over in her mind when Reg's plaintive calls for help brought her back to the present. She was mad, quite mad. She should be running after Libby and begging her to marry Mackenzie instead of letting him run around loose. Emma hurried backstage and walked right into a mass of pink carnations and trembling, fairy-like, white gypsophila. Her premonitions sharpened as the massive tribute swayed sideways and a grinning face emerged behind it.

'G'day, Emma,' Wayne Sweet said.

CHAPTER TEN

HE DOGGED her steps until the show was under way. No amount of polite explanation that she was busy seemed to penetrate his skull. He wanted to know if she had received his marriage proposal and Emma almost told him she'd thrown the latest one in the bin with the rest of the junk mail. Something told her that this would only incite him to produce yet another proposal. 'I'm already engaged,' she said instead, grinding her teeth that she had to resort to this.

The grin wavered a bit. 'To the big bloke?' he said. 'The one who was boss of the firefighters in Catastrophe?'

Emma stared. 'What makes you think it's him?'

'I saw him at your house today.'

People were milling all around but Emma felt a chill little sensation down her spine. 'You were at my house?' she said coldly.

'You might change your mind about him,' Wayne said with obtuse persistence.

'I won't,' she said with conviction. 'He's the only man for me.'

Wayne had disappeared by the time the show had finished. But later, she found the pink carnations crushed into a waste-bin. A spray of gypsophila survived unmarred, trembling in the breeze of the passing stage crew. Emma looked at it uneasily, remembering the phrase that had persuaded Wayne to give up. He's the only man for me. It repeated in her mind, gaining resonance. She should never have said the words, she thought, not even to get rid of Wayne. Words said out loud took on a life of their own. An actress ought to know that.

The cleaners came and went. The stage crew including Steve, left, and Emma stayed on alone to plan the next day's work. It was something she often did, taking advantage of the peace and quiet of early morning when no phones rang and there was no one to interrupt save the night-watchman when he came on duty. Tonight, she admitted, she was postponing going home. Logically, she knew Mackenzie would not be still sprawled on her bed twelve hours later, but the image of him there had driven her to find excuses to work late, to delay the moment when she had to sleep in her bed again, knowing he had been there. He's the only man for me. . . The phrase kept popping up in her thoughts, with a nagging few bars of Spanish folk music. She disciplined herself to concentrate on her work. It was one in the morning when she smelled smoke.

Emma sniffed the air and went back to work. It was the leftover smell from the green room, the only place she allowed smoking backstage, she decided. The smoke alarms would go off if it was anything else. Minutes later, a wisp of smoke curled around her doorway. Emma shot to her feet, registering that the smell was too sharp for stale smoke. She hurried into the corridor. The lights were haloed with smoke, the stairs indistinct. She lugged a fire extinguisher from the wall. Why weren't the alarms going?

Smoke poured from the store-room and Emma's heart sank. Costumes, spare sets and building materials, paint and turpentine—it was a cocktail of flammable materials. When she looked in it didn't look too bad and she advanced, hugging the extinguisher under one arm, spraying in a semi-circle over a heap of smouldering cloth. But even as she thought things could be worse, things got worse. A bottle burst and flame exploded over a pool of paint-thinner and spread to a rack crammed with costumes. Emma was driven back to the door by the heat. 'Got to hunch down,' she panted, remembering Mackenzie's advice on heat radiation. Mackenzie would know what to do. The flames streamed out towards her and the source of oxygen in the corridor and Emma backed off, yelling, 'Mackenzie!' or 'Help!' she wasn't quite sure which.

She heard heavy footsteps overhead, running. A crashing on the stairs and, through the pall of smoke, a solid shape materialising. Emma gaped, thinking she'd dreamed him up. 'Mackenzie?' She pawed at his fabulous chest, grateful for the substance of her dreams. 'It's a fire,' she said inanely.

'Well, let's put the damned thing out, Emma,' he said.

They had the fire almost out by the time the fire brigade arrived. Throats dry, eyes reddened, Emma and Mackenzie sat outside the back entrance where the fire engine lights flashed and a cluster of night people and street kids watched. 'How did you know I was here?' Mackenzie asked, grimacing over the mug of heavily sugared tea someone had made.

'I didn't.'

His profile flickered in the whirling brigade light like an image on an old silent movie. Such a strong face, he had. It would look the same in thirty years' time, she thought. He turned to look at her. 'But you called my name, Emma.'

'Oh—I thought I yelled for help.'

'"Mackenzie" was what you yelled.'

'Oh. Well,' she said, shrugging. 'Same thing.' She looked sharply at him then, realising what she'd said. For someone who had vowed not to rely on a man it was almost treason, she thought. Mackenzie of course, was pleased, complacent even.

As she sat there beside him and the smoke-daze

wore off, she frowned at the oddity of it. 'What on earth *were* you doing here, Mackenzie? The last time I saw you, you were asleep——'

He smiled reminiscently. 'On your bed. It smelled of you.'

Emma gave a harried little shake of her head. 'Of course it didn't.'

'The smell of your hair on the pillow—I had a dream. . .' The reminiscent smile deepened. She frowned, feeling a certain anxiety as to how she might have performed in his dreams.

'So what were you doing here in the theatre?' she demanded, reflecting that she could hardly act more idiotically in his dreams than in real life.

'I've been here since the show ended. I must have missed him,' he said grimly.

'Missed who?'

'Your firebug.'

Emma's mouth opened and shut. 'What do you mean?'

A police car drew up then and several of the onlookers just faded away into the night. Two policemen got out and came towards Emma and Mackenzie.

'It was arson, Emma. The fires are still following you around.'

The arsonist was Wayne. Days later, Emma still felt bad about it.

'As if,' she said to Ami over lunch in her own cluttered kitchen, 'the fires are *my* fault for just attracting Wayne's attention.' Wayne was picked up by the police that same night and she'd seen him at the police station when she and Mackenzie had attended to the formalities of laying charges.

'Oh, Emma,' Wayne Sweet had said reproachfully. 'I loved you. Why couldn't you like me just a little bit? I never would have done it if you'd been nice to me.'

And so young and downcast did he look in his unrequited love that even the police seemed to sympathise with him. They shot little glances at her and she felt she was somehow coming out of this as some wanton woman playing with men's emotions, driving them to crime. The young and downcast Wayne had coldly disabled the smoke alarm system and set a fire that could have burned the whole theatre down and killed her. Nevertheless, all that loss and destruction and heartbreak settled on her in a burden of guilt. At the same time she was angry that she should feel some sense of responsibility. 'What am I supposed to do?' she burst out in anguish. 'Say yes to every selfish, pestering male just in case he goes out and burns down a town?'

Mackenzie took her hand. 'You aren't responsible,' he said. 'He's a spoiled tyrant who couldn't accept no for an answer.'

Emma snatched her hand away. 'That's not what you seemed to think in the past! You sympathised with poor Wayne when I said I kept telling him I didn't want his flowers and attentions. You—you acted as if I was a—a man-trap causing trouble wherever I went, relishing having a man *adoring* me. A natural disaster personified! You blamed *me* for the way *you* felt. You might put out fires instead of starting them, Mackenzie, but as far as I can see you're a lot like him!'

And Mackenzie, she remembered, had looked shocked and grim. His eyes had turned icy and he hadn't spoken to her again that night. Steve, summoned by Mackenzie, had driven her home.

'I told him off,' she said to Ami now. 'He'll probably never speak to me again.'

'Wayne Sweet?' Ami said, puzzled.

'No. Mackenzie. He just disappeared. Steve hasn't seen him either. I should have said thank you, I suppose. He was waiting in the theatre just to—look

out for me. If nothing had happened I wouldn't have
known he was there. . .' Emma was unused to being
watched over and she didn't quite like it, but she didn't
quite dislike it, either. Mackenzie, he'd told the police,
had seen a car parked outside her place when he'd left
that morning. A car with a man in it and a large bunch
of pink carnations on the back seat. Although he knew
Wayne was under suspicion, he'd never seen the man,
but he'd remembered what she'd said about the nuisance fan with pink flowers and doubled back, but the
car had gone. She rested her hand in her chin and
wondered about a man who didn't have to brag about
taking action to protect her, but had simply, quietly
done it. The kind of man who didn't have to have his
own name up in lights.

'You love him,' Ami said, pouring more wine. 'I
suspected it might come to this when I got your first
postcard.'

Emma blinked but didn't argue. I love him, she
thought. What's news? 'But I hardly said anything
about him in that postcard—only that he was an
arrogant male chauvinist pig.'

Ami grinned. 'My intuition was working overtime.
Matt is more than a little fond of you, too, old pal.
That time in my shop—his hands kept clenching every
time Libby mentioned your name.'

Emma laughed shakily. 'Oh, well, that's conclusive!'

'So where do you go from here?'

Emma looked around at her own familiar home,
cluttered with her collected treasures of the past four
years, and felt that sense of something missing. 'I
couldn't risk it again, Ami. You remember what it was
like with Simon? I almost disappeared as a person
because he was so good at making things happen the
way he wanted them. And believe me, Mackenzie
makes Simon look like a little kid playing with his toys.

He's used to being the boss. Used to people doing what *he* wants——'

Ami snorted. 'So—there's this gorgeous man—gets his hair burned off for you and gets told off after he's played Phantom of the Opera to protect you and you're going to let him go because you're frightened he might take over your life? For heaven's sake, Emma—you're not the insecure girl you were when you married Simon. You're more than a match for a boss man now. You're a boss woman, aren't you? You're used to people doing what you want, too, otherwise you'd never keep a theatre running in a city with a cinema on every corner. Tell me this: have you ever once yet lain down and let Mackenzie walk over you like a doormat?'

Emma smiled, thinking that the battle honours were fairly even. 'No.'

'Well then.'

'But where might it lead? If it was marriage, I couldn't do it.' She swallowed. 'Not again.'

Ami shrugged. 'You're jumping the gun, aren't you? Why don't you just have a raging affair and see how it goes?'

As she was leaving, Ami turned to her and said, 'You're mad if you don't take him. He's good-looking, single, mature and hetero.'

Emma laughed. 'Ami!'

'And he's *tall*,' she said by way of a clincher. 'From one five-foot-tenner to another, I leave you with that thought.'

This particular tall man had vanished into the blue. According to Steve, Mackenzie had phoned once and said he was spending some time with John and Libby Crawford before he went back to Catastrophe, offering moral support while John saw more doctors. That was four days ago. So much for *taking* Mackenzie, Emma thought. Perhaps John Crawford had had his hope

realised that Libby and Mackenzie would get back
together.

On a May day of lowering clouds and chill, late
autumn winds, Emma gave herself the challenge of a
turquoise day. She saw some glints of it in the choppy
grey-green waters of the harbour, an arc of it in a
fading rainbow, iridescent streaks of it in oil slicks on
wet roads. The theatre was to be closed that night and
Emma left her office around four. She drove home but
on impulse, reversed out of the drive again and drove
down to the beach. She thought she saw a truck with
faded patches of red on it but she was always seeing
trucks like that. She was supposed to be looking for
turquoise. Not faded red. Nor green.

The sands of Bondi were criss-crossed by footprints.
In the most dismal weather, hardy surfers surfed,
joggers jogged, walkers walked and dog-lovers exer-
cised their pets. She was almost down to the water's
edge when something made her look back. There,
framed on the famous beach pavilion, was Mackenzie.
He came down the steps and toward her, steaming
along at such a pace that she thought he must be
furious but as he came nearer, he slowed. If it was
anyone but Mackenzie she would have thought he'd
grown suddenly hesitant. The pounding of her heart
mingled with the roar of the surf. He wore jeans and a
sweater under the tweedy jacket she remembered.
He'd shaved and his hair was windblown and spiked
over his forehead. He looked grim and remote, with
his wide-screen reflector sunglasses giving her a distorted panorama of Bondi Beach. Perhaps, she thought
wildly, he had totted up all that fire damage and come
to tell her it wouldn't have happened if only she'd been
nice to Wayne. Perhaps he'd just called to tell her it
was all pre-wedding nerves and he was getting married
next week after all. Perhaps he was here to say
goodbye, again. The surf pounded in her ears.

'How did you know I was here?' she asked, marvelling at the human brain that could deal out such prosaic gems while it grappled with life-shattering issues.

'I was waiting at your house. Followed you,' he said abruptly. His voice was rough.

'I meant to thank you, Mackenzie,' she said. 'For helping me at the theatre. . .everything.'

He made a dismissive little gesture. 'You said some things that night at the police station that I've thought over. You were right.' It sounded flat and rehearsed, something to be dispensed with quickly. 'I've always thought of myself as steady and reliable. Mature. When you came along and I began to think and act like a jealous, fickle adolescent—I didn't like it.' Nothing conciliatory about it. Nothing apologetic. More the tone of a man putting the record straight simply because his integrity had been questioned. The salt-wind went right through her clothes. A few raindrops plopped on the sand.

'It was as if I was under a spell,' Mackenzie said and she almost laughed. He looked and sounded like a robot—admirably spell-resistant. 'And I looked around for reasons that would make me feel it was just a temporary lapse.'

'And you decided *I* was the reason!' she said with asperity. 'A wicked woman with mystical powers who *made* you think dishonourable thoughts. Just as I'm supposed to have *made* Wayne so forlorn he had to set half the country on fire. For heaven's sake, Mackenzie. They used to burn women as witches for feeble reasons like that!'

His mouth hardened. 'I thought about what you said. And I did see some similarities between myself and Wayne,' he said with distaste. 'I apologise, for what it's worth.'

She was taken aback. It was worth quite a lot, she thought, seeing the genuine self-scrutiny Mackenzie was putting himself through. Simon had been much addicted to glib apology but not given at all to self-scrutiny.

'While we're on the subject of Wayne and the fires,' he said in that same rehearsed tone, 'I want you to believe that I didn't seriously ever think you were the one lighting fires. I—let myself dwell on the possibility simply because—well—I had a responsibility to consider it and I couldn't let my—attraction to you cloud the issue. But it was never any more than the vaguest suspicion. By the time I spoke to the police, they were already following up on a description of Wayne from a witness.'

'Well,' Emma said, briskly. 'I'm glad that's cleared up.'

'Look,' Mackenzie said. 'We haven't known each other very long.'

She'd been longing to hear a softer note in his voice. This one stung like the sand being flung by the wind. And the phrasing had all the hallmarks of the round-about goodbye. Explanations, followed by apologies, followed by some philosophical regrets, followed by goodbye. A therapeutic way to tidy up all the loose ends of a hot November. 'Long enough,' she said, continuing her walk along the beach to nowhere in particular.

'We haven't exactly hit it off together——'

She snorted. 'You can say that again, Mackenzie!'

Mackenzie's mouth compressed. 'But you can't deny there's something between us.'

'Are you asking me or telling me?' she yelled above the wind, picking up her pace to fairly lope over the sand.

'Why can't you admit it? You like to think you're so honest and up-front, Emma, but you're not. You accused me of dishonesty, and you were right, but you aren't so full of integrity yourself.' He grabbed her arm and jerked her to a stop. She looked into his sunglasses and saw two reflections of herself in false companionship, when she was wan and lonely. 'The moment I was free, you were looking for excuses to back off, but in Catastrophe, when you thought I was to be safely married to someone else, you could hardly keep your hands off me.'

Red-faced, she took a swipe at him, but he ducked. 'Hit a nerve, did I?' he drawled.

'You know you did,' she snapped. 'You're exaggerating of course because your ego's so overgrown—I kept my hands off you *dozens* of times when I would have liked to——' His mouth dropped open and she went on hastily, 'But I *did* feel happier about you when you were a safe proposition and I *did* feel like running a mile when you turned up free as a bird. I didn't think I could handle a boss man on the loose. I admit it, see? But that was *last week*!' As she said it, she thought it might as well have been a year ago.

Mackenzie's hand bit into her arm. 'And—this week?'

'This week,' she said huskily, 'I think maybe I *could* handle a boss man on the loose.' Talk about jumping through fire, she thought panicking. Was she crazy? Have a raging affair, Ami had said. An affair that would last only as long as passion was more important than distance. 'But of course, it's ridiculous—I run a theatre, you run cattle! You live out west hundreds of miles away, and I live——' she made a vague sweeping gesture that turned the metropolis of Sydney into a village '—over there.'

He hadn't moved a muscle, hadn't uttered a word, and Emma shivered and wrapped her arms around her as the wind brought up goose-bumps on her skin. 'Are you ever going to speak again, Mackenzie?' she snapped, fearful that she'd made a prize fool of herself.

It might have been only goodbye he'd come for, after all.

He took off his jacket and offered it to her. Emma's temper sizzled. It wasn't gallantry she wanted, but some response now that she'd bared her soul. 'No, thanks.'

He came towards her with the coat held open. Like a bullfighter with a cape, she thought riotously. In his sunglasses she saw a bland stretch of sand and a Bondi beach wanderer with a metal detector. I hope she's detecting more than I am, Emma thought. Furious, she snatched the sunglasses off. 'If you won't speak, then at least let me *see* what you're thinking——'

And, standing close to him, she did see. 'Mackenzie——' she whispered at the look in his eyes. He put his coat around her shoulders, drew her into his arms and held her tightly to him, not moving at all while the wind plucked at their hair and their clothes and the sea washed onto the shore again and again. The rain was falling gently now, invisible drops making dots on the sand.

'The first time I saw rain I couldn't get a word out for about ten minutes,' he said at last. 'The best things in life, the beautiful things, get me like that.'

'Oh, Mackenzie, I love you——' she said, laughing and crying and remembering some of his silences. 'It's worth waiting to hear you speak.'

He kissed her, softly, tenderly while he found his voice, and when he said, 'I love you, Emma,' it was as if she'd already heard it. 'I tried to tell myself it was just chemistry. That's what happens when you've waited for something and you think you'll never find it—either you devalue it, you say, well it can't be as good as everyone says. Or you talk yourself into thinking you've found it. The way I did with Libby.' He gazed out to sea. 'I was—am very fond of her, Emma. At the time I might have been vaguely aware that I was trying to whip up a dimension to fondness that just wasn't there, but it wasn't until I met you——' He looked up, held out his hands to the rain. 'People try to describe it, but you never know what it's like until you've experienced the real thing.'

The rain grew heavier and they stood there as it drenched them, smiling at each other. 'When it rains, it pours,' he said, reminding her of the day in the cave when she thought he might have been saying something else. The smiles turned into laughter and the laughter wouldn't stop. Mackenzie threw out his arms and spun around in the rain, fell flat on his back and opened his mouth to taste the raindrops. And Emma, falling down with him, kissed him and tasted raindrops too. He rolled over pinning her to the sand. 'I've got nowhere to sleep tonight.'

'Tch, tch. You could bunk in with Steve.'

'No spare bed.'

'There's your truck.'

'Too cold.'

She considered. 'I could give you permission to sleep in the theatre.'

'Touché,' he said, lips twitching. 'But I'm holding out for a better offer. Now that you feel you can handle me, would you please take me home and handle me?'

'I suppose you could stay at my place,' she said breathlessly. 'But no more of that kinky stuff in the mirror.'

His green eyes gleamed. 'Emma, my love,' he said indulgently, 'that wasn't kinky.'

'Creative,' Mackenzie murmured a little while later. 'Not kinky.' Their wet clothes, coated with sand, lay on the bathroom floor. The shower streamed over them, steam swirled and Emma's philodendrons looked like jungle plants in the tropical humidity. Mackenzie held her breasts, lifted them, sipped and suckled and murmured his admiration, and for Emma it was heaven except for the occasional glimpses she saw in the mirror when she opened her eyes unwarily. Mackenzie saw her looking away and she said huskily, 'I've always been self-conscious about—my size.'

He turned her so that she couldn't avoid the mirror and took her hands, held them to her breasts, inviting her to appreciate this part of herself as he did. 'Part of you, Emma. A lovely part.' In the mirror, she saw the flash of his smile behind her as he made a sensual little pass with his hands and hers. 'A *big* part.' And she was laughing and craving his touch, catching back his hands when mercifully the steam obscured the image of her own naked enjoyment. He knelt and rinsed soap from her legs, his large hands slithering up over her thighs to flex on her buttocks, angling her body for his kiss. Emma drove her hands into her hair and she heard a deep-throated sigh come muffled out of the mist, like a primitive sound from a jungle before she recognised it as her own. And the water rained and rained. . .in time it was she who knelt and marvelled and Mackenzie who growled his pleasure. Emma laughed in elation at this lover of hers who went weak at the knees when she held him in her hands and who took such care to pleasure her.

And later, on her bed, with lamplight playing softly over them, he said, 'You're going to love this, my beautiful Amazon,' then kept her breathlessly waiting until she took matters into her own hands. 'Emma——' he sighed, and she thought he muttered something about her being a witch after all before he gathered her up and stroked her legs apart. And she held his big, powerful body and cried out her delight when he entered her. 'Oh, I do,' she gasped, looking into his eyes. 'I do love it.'

Mackenzie grinned wickedly. 'Emma, my love—not that.' He rolled his hips. '*This*——'

* * *

Emma couldn't stop smiling. Dreamily, she watched Mackenzie tuck into a pile of sandwiches they had made from fridge leftovers.

'You look very——' he said, grinning at her.

'Very what?'

'Satisfied.' And he looked supremely complacent, sitting there wrapped again in one of her apricot towels.

'I'm an actress,' she said. 'I might be pretending.'

Mackenzie eyed her challengingly. 'We'll put it to the test again some time.'

And though she tried, she couldn't disguise her quick indrawn breath of anticipation, nor the visible response of her body beneath the silk robe. Mackenzie laughed and demolished a cheese sandwich.

'I'm an old-fashioned man. Will you marry me?' he said.

Emma was silent for so long that he turned red. 'For God's sake, Emma—that's *not* a rhetorical question. I know I could have said that better—but you're supposed to say *something*.'

'I'm a new-fashioned woman. I have reservations about marriage.' She looked him in the eye. 'I did warn you.'

His expression could have been carved out of stone. 'So you did. Just how deep do these reservations run?'

'I don't want to get married.'

He leaned back and folded his arms, staring at her as if she'd said she was an alien. 'That is fairly deep,' he said sardonically. 'And how were you envisaging our relationship would go on from here, Emma? An everlasting affair? Nookie on long weekends and bank holidays? Will you pop out west to sleep with your lover? Will I come to the city for a quickie with my mistress? Will we chip in for tea and coffee expenses?'

'Well, what were *you* expecting?' she flung back. 'To just replace one bride with another? If you'd proposed a bit quicker, you could have kept the same booking at the church!'

His jaw clenched so hard that white lines appeared around his mouth. 'I know you and your friends probably think it's trendy but I'm not interested in some bohemian set-up, Emma. I'm thirty-two. I want to settle down. I want some family life. What exactly have you got against marriage, except that it's bourgeois and too, too tame for theatrical types?'

Family life, she thought, seeing in her mind's eye Mackenzie holding a baby, chasing a laughing child. Part of her yearned for it, but another, bruised and cautious part said, What if it doesn't work?

'Perhaps you should have checked whether I can have children, then,' she said savagely. 'What *you* want is a package deal. I'm only offering me.'

He looked staggered. 'You can't have children?' he said.

Her face flamed. 'Well, I didn't say I *couldn't*, just that if it's so damned important to you you should have found out first if I was able—and willing—to fulfil all these plans *you* have!' And she could see by his face what a blow it would be if she couldn't, or wouldn't. It wasn't going to work, she'd known all along it wouldn't she thought, agonised. 'You can't say I didn't warn you,' she said again, defensively.

'No, I can't,' he bit out. 'You wouldn't give up your name, your house and your job for a man, you said. I suppose I thought you might make some compromise for a man you loved. You did say you loved me? I didn't realise it was conditional.'

'Isn't yours conditional, then?' she flared. 'Conditional on *me* doing things your way? As for compromises, Mackenzie, I know all about them!' She went to a chest of drawers in her living-room, opened the bottom one and withdrew a wrapped parcel. She unwound a length of black fabric from it and revealed a framed photograph. She held it to her chest a moment, took a deep breath, then thrust the picture at Mackenzie. 'That's what I've got against getting married.'

Matt took it reluctantly, some sixth sense telling him he wasn't going to like this. It was a wedding photograph. Emma, dressed in lace, veiled in white. A younger Emma, hauntingly lovely with her hair a riot of curls around her face, her smile incandescent. He felt the gut-wrench of jealously at that smile—the innocence and the naïveté of it. Beside her, a man in a grey morning suit with a burgundy ascot. A handsome man, triumphant, possessive. Behind them a church. Matt felt as if he'd been king-hit. 'You never said you'd been married. . .this is Simon?'

She nodded, clasping and unclasping her hands.

'You talked about it as if you'd just lived together.'

'We *did* live together,' she said sharply. 'We were married first. Very traditional. Nothing bohemian. Lots of compromises. I gave up—almost everything he wanted me to, but almost was never enough. We were married for two years before we were divorced. What I have against marriage is that I tried it and it didn't work and I never want to fail—feel like that again.' She laid her hand on the back of a chair and raised her head to a resolute angle. 'I'm sorry,' she added in a low voice.

'Sorry!' he snapped, before he could stop himself. He glared at the photograph, jealous of the man, jealous of that uncomplicated giving-in Emma. He hadn't imagined that she'd been wildly in love with the fellow Simon, the way she'd talked. He'd pictured it comfortably as a minor affair, not this! Emma was his first true love, but he was not hers. He felt desolate, helpless. Second-best. It was a new experience for him. He'd always been the best, first, always assumed that

this was somehow the natural order of things. What
was he going to do now? He felt murderous. He
gripped the picture, wanted to smash it. But he saw
Emma's white face and tossed it on a chair instead.
With luck the bloody thing would bounce off and break
accidentally. What a shame. But it didn't.

'I think I'd better go,' he said heavily.

It took him only two hours of walking on the beach
before he came back. She needn't have shown him the
picture, he realised. It was unlikely that she showed it
to anyone else. Strong, independent Emma Spencer
kept that picture—not casually on display with her
others, but hidden in a bottom drawer, shrouded in
black. It had been a struggle for her to hand it to him
and reveal so much about herself. Emma Spencer, he
decided, was ashamed of the sweet, naïve girl in that
photograph. She never wanted to feel like that again.
Or had she said *fail*? Emma didn't like to fail, he knew.
Remember her defensiveness whenever he'd made a
crack about her leadership and the disloyalty of her
crew? He loved her. What the hell was he going to do?
He'd always thought when he found the woman he
wanted he'd have a plan, a logical outcome. Matt's
logical outcomes shattered like the surf into a million
scraps of foam. He turned into the wind and went back
to her.

She opened the door and he felt the leap of his heart,
his body. 'Are you free on long weekends and bank
holidays?' he said wryly and she came into his arms
and held him and surrounded him with her generous
warmth and he thought that there could be worse
things than a lifetime affair with Emma.

The months slipped by. May, June. Mackenzie had a
week's holiday in Sydney. July, August. Emma took a
few days off and went to Catastrophe, Mackenzie spent
a weekend in the city. Emma's life was hectic, differ-

ent. Mackenzie physically came and went in it but thoughts of him stayed with her, made an empty space where there had been none. In Sydney they wandered around the city, listened to jazz on the harbour, visited galleries, made love in Emma's bed. In Catastrophe they rode to stark, beautiful places where there was no sound but insects and birds, went to a rodeo, flew over the country where the bushfire's burns were gradually softened by new growth. The centenary celebrations, scaled down from lack of funds, were to be held in November, a year late. Emma and her crew were invited to come back for the commemorative performance in the Amphitheatre. To her surprise, Bernie, Alison and Reg said they would go.

'The performance *is* in a cave, remember,' she warned them.

'Just see if you can keep the bats offstage, there's a love,' Bernie said.

Mackenzie paid his union dues and on busy nights in the theatre moved scenery and made coffee. Emma learned about cattle drench and ticks and worms. Mackenzie shuffled his farm journals so that she had a place for the manuscripts she took with her to his place. She had a spring-clean in late August and threw out some of her collected bits and pieces to make space on the shelves for Mackenzie's books. She unwrapped her wedding photo and put it with several others that captured parts of her life. She wrinkled her nose at the picture, feeling a distant affection for Simon that was all that was left after years of resentment and self-recrimination. Simon had been weak in many ways but she had made it easy for him to manipulate her. She'd learned a lot from him and really, on the whole, she was grateful. It stopped Mackenzie in his tracks when he saw the photograph with the others.

'I was emptying out that drawer for your jazz tapes,'

she said, shrugging. 'And I didn't know where else to put it. Does it bother you?'

'Yes, it bloody bothers me,' he said, curling his lip at Simon. 'The man looks like Byron and Mel Gibson rolled into one.'

Emma laughed. 'Poor Simon, he was always good to look at, I'll say that for him.'

'That sounds like an epitaph,' Mackenzie said, with a gleam in his eyes.

'Does it?' she said, without much interest. 'Anyway, the drawer is empty now if you want to store your tapes there.'

'This is ridiculous,' Mackenzie grumbled. 'Half my tapes back home, half down here. I have to come to Sydney whenever I want to hear my favourite Miles Davis tracks.'

Emma's eyes sparkled. 'Is that why you come here so often?'

'That—and other favourite things.' Mackenzie pulled her into his arms and kissed her and she wasn't sure why he seemed so triumphant.

But the distance couldn't be joked away. It was inconvenient, having belongings in two places. It was unsatisfactory, always saying goodbye. It was tiring, always packing and unpacking. The gaps between their times together lengthened. Mackenzie began to spend more time with his brother when he visited and she often found herself watching them kick a soccer ball around her front lawn.

'You and Steve are finally acting like brothers instead of stern parent and rebellious child,' she observed, after a Sunday afternoon of watching them lope around like children.

'He had the right idea,' Mackenzie said ruefully. 'Taking off the way he did so often. We needed to get out from under each other's feet for a while. If I'd been smarter I would have seen it for what it was instead of——'

He chewed his lip and Emma prompted, 'Instead of what?'

'I—suspected him of being the firebug.'

'Steve?' she said, startled. But then she remembered Steve saying, 'She's beautiful, isn't she?' about the fire that first day. A haggard Mackenzie, asking her if she'd seen his brother on the day of the Catastrophe fire. 'Why haven't you told me this?'

'I'm not proud of it,' he said grimly. 'I'd been worried about him for some time. The disappearances—his attitude. And he'd set fire to a shed when he was fifteen, just larking around, but when I started keeping that chart and realised his disappearances coincided with the fire dates I started to wonder if——' He made a sheepish gesture with one hand. 'That was one reason, I suppose, that I let myself believe *you* could be involved. I was ready to seize on any alternative rather than believe my brother was doing it.'

'And the other reason?'

'I convinced myself that I couldn't fall for a woman who would do such things. *Ergo*—if I could establish that you were that kind of woman, I wouldn't fall for you.' He gave a sigh of resignation. 'Bloody futile. My only excuse is that I was in a blue funk. Trying to arm myself against your power, my love.'

'You could have tied garlic around your neck,' she said acerbically.

'Would that have kept you away?' he asked, opening his eyes wide.

'So all that detached reasoning in your study that night—all that "everywhere you went there's been a fire" stuff—was you in a blue funk?' Emma said.

He hooted. 'Detached reasoning! I haven't done any of that since the hottest November in sixty years. That was me pretending to be Sherlock Holmes to stop thinking about throwing you down on my couch and unwrapping you from that silky thing you were wearing and spreading those delectable——'

'Mackenzie!' she said, reddening.

'—arms out wide so that I could get at——'

'Mackenzie!'

'—that lovely neck of yours.'

And he'd sleepily pulled her to him and held her arms out wide and kissed her neck and other favourite places. 'The trouble with you, Mackenzie,' she'd whispered in his ear, 'is you never know when to stop.'

'I tell you what. I'll just go ahead and you say when,' he suggested. But she forgot to say when.

September. Emma cancelled a weekend in Catastrophe because she was exhausted after a heavy week. Mackenzie said he wouldn't be able to leave his place not until after the Centenary celebrations. When Emma and her crew drove into Catastrophe, she hadn't seen him for seven weeks.

Catastrophe looked very much like the other country towns they'd passed through. The burned houses had been rebuilt, the community hall repaired. Along the main street of town, the multi-coloured flags were up again and some of the rosebushes bloomed. In Col Mundy's pub, the plastic palm trees reigned in plenty as they had in drought.

'Yep, everything back to normal,' Col Mundy confirmed when Bernie asked about the burned out homesteads. 'Nobody sold up. Everyone rebuilt.'

'You're all crazy,' Bernie said, shaking his head. 'You ought to run like hell to a safer place. There are no guarantee it won't happen again.'

Col gave his grave-digger's smile. 'No guarantees I'll have a reservation for you this time, but you've turned up to try again, eh?'

No guarantees, Emma thought as she waited out the front of the pub for Mackenzie. He'd said he would meet her there but she didn't know if he was flying or driving in. Not a thing moved except the flags until a vehicle appeared in the distance. Emma shaded her eyes and watched it, her heart beating out a ragged rhythm. The truck tore down Catastrophe's main street with a deep-throated roar and screeched to a stop in one of a dozen empty parking spaces. A big man got out and crushed a hat on to his head, slammed the truck door and steamed toward the pub. No guarantee for rebuilding. But a safer place could be very unsatisfying.

He hadn't seen her yet and Emma watched him, noticing the tension in his big shoulders, the deliberation of his stride. I could lose this man, she thought, feeling the panic rise in her. I could never hold him in my arms again or hear that voice murmuring wicked things in my ear. She looked down the street of Catastrophe and thought her life could be like that. A long emptiness stretching out to a hazy horizon, just a few flags flickering as a reminder of fleeting moments of glory. Mackenzie stopped abruptly and turned to the garden strip in the centre of the street. He glanced up and down the street, then hunched over, and a rosebush trembled violently. Emma heard him curse, then he took a penknife from his pocket and hacked at a stem. He turned back towards the pub with a white rose in his hand.

She gave a shaky laugh and tears ran down her face. Emma wiped them away and went to meet him. Mackenzie stopped still and stared at her. The white rose bobbed in a warm breeze.

He looked narrowly at the glisten of tears on her cheeks.

'Before you say anything,' he said grimly, as if he'd rehearsed it, 'I can't stand this any more and I've made a few decisions——'

'But I wanted to tell you—I've been approached by

someone for a long lease and if the investors agree it's
a good proposition it would mean I was free for six
months. I'd like to submit a proposition to develop a
theatre based on a cave—a real underground theatre—
that way I could live with you——'

'I'm applying to the university in Sydney to take up
my studies again. Matt's going to get his chance to run
Falkners for a couple of years and that means I
can——' he stopped, belatedly registering what she'd
said, and finished huskily '—live with you. '

They stood there just looking at each other. Eventually, Mackenzie held out the rose to her. The way he'd
held out his jacket to her on the beach. It wasn't just
what Mackenzie *said*, Emma thought tremulously. His
silences truly could be golden.

'I saw you pick it. And you a councillor,' she said
huskily, sniffing the fragrance of the contraband rose.
The bush was still trembling from Mackenzie's attentions. She was trembling in anticipation of them. He
took her hand and led her to the truck.

'It's a long way to your place,' she commented.

Mackenzie gave a wolfish grin. 'But it's my secretary's day off,' he said, and it was only a minute later
that he parked outside his office. He groaned. Joyce's
four-wheel drive was there.

'If it isn't the long-distance lovers,' Joyce said,
kissing Emma. 'I just dropped in with the awards for
your lot.'

'My lot?' Emma said. 'What awards?'

'Community service during the bushfire,' Joyce told
her. 'You get one each.' And she waved towards four
J. Clements paintings, uniformly awful, lined up
against the wall. She grinned at Emma, who was just
beginning to appreciate the irony. 'Which one do you
think the galloping gourmet will hate the most?'

'Joyce,' Mackenzie said, steering her to the door. 'I
love you. Go away. We have things to do.'

'I'll bring a basket of goodies for breakfast tomorrow,' she said with a leer, '"Oh, who's afraid of the big, bad wolf——"' she sang as the door closed on her. Mackenzie leaned back on the door and looked at Emma, taking in every little detail from her leather lace-ups to her hair, braided high.

'My best friend,' Emma said, 'told me I'd be a fool not to take you.'

'Well. You *took* me,' he said with a reminiscent look in his eye. He took off his hat and tossed it onto his desk. Slowly, he came over to her. She reached out and touched his face, loving the craggy jut of his nose, the ambiguous lines of his mouth, the hard shape of his jaw. His eyes closed and he reached for her, pulling her close with a mighty sigh. 'I've missed you,' he muttered into her neck.

'I missed you. I've put on weight.'

'Shouldn't you lose weight when you're pining?'

'All that chocolate cake,' she mourned. 'Home-baked bread rolls—I had to do something. I was miserable.

'Good. When and how can we move in together? I don't care where—your place or mine.'

'Let it be on the ranch. It's where we first fell in love and it's where I want to be.'

Mackenzie straightened and looked carefully at her. 'You wouldn't give up your name, your job, your house for a man, you said.'

'I'm—not as attached to it as I thought. And I'm more attached to you than I thought.'

There was a gleam in his green eyes. 'And I fell in love with a theatre director and I'm not asking you to give up your job,' he said. 'That only leaves your name.'

'I'd like to keep that,' she said, smiling at him.

Mackenzie's eyes narrowed. 'I see.'

'I think I started to fall in love with you when I

realised you'd put Gertrude's name over your gate.
I've never met another man who wouldn't prefer his
own name up in lights.'

He gave a rueful smile.

'Do you mind? It's just that we bohemian theatre
types tend to keep our own names when we marry.'

His head came up. '*Marry*? When you said keep
your own name, I thought. . .you said you never
wanted to marry again.'

'Yes, but that was in *April*,' she said.

Mackenzie grinned, his eyes glinting with satisfaction. 'If you think I'm going to propose again and risk
being rejected, forget it.'

'This from the man who took me through a wall of
flame,' she said sorrowfully. 'I suppose I'll have to
make do with the memories of that very prosaic
proposal you made—over a cheese sandwich.'

Mackenzie smiled, brushed the backs of his fingers
down the side of her face. 'I love you, Emma Spencer.
Can I marry you and be your love? Will you marry me,
and be mine?'

'Yes and yes,' she said, and kissed him.

'You realise that it won't matter what *you* decide—
folks in these parts will call you Mrs Mackenzie,' he
said.

'And in Sydney, some people will probably call you
Mr Spencer. How will you feel about that?'

He bent and lifted her in his arms. 'I can live with
it.'

Emma's face fell. 'Oh, but what about the kids?'

Mackenzie frowned. 'I want some, but if you don't,
then——'

'No, no,' she said urgently. 'I *want* some but it just
occurred to me—what will we call *them*?'

He laughed and laid her on the divan. Mackenzie
was looking very pleased, confident, very complacent.
A beautiful, challenging, dangerous man. A loving

man. Emma ran her hand along the lovely, rugged line of his shoulder and arm, smiling. Her own confidence soared.

'We have some negotiating to do, Emma Spencer,' he said.

'Are you good at negotiating, Mackenzie?' she enquired, as if she didn't know.

His green eyes glinted as he leaned over her, traced a finger down her braided hair. 'I usually get what I want.'

'So do I,' she said, smiling. Emma put her arms around his neck and looked deep in his eyes. She sighed. 'What a lovely day.'

She was having a green day.

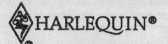

HARLEQUIN PRESENTS®

Don't be late for the wedding!

Be sure to make a date in your diary for the happy event—
the sixth in our tantalizing new selection of stories...

Wedlocked!

Bonded in matrimony, torn by desire...

Coming next month:

THE YULETIDE BRIDE by Mary Lyons
(Harlequin Presents #1781)

From the celebrated author of *Dark and Dangerous*

A Christmas wedding should be the most romantic of
occasions. But when Max asked Amber to be his
Yuletide Bride, romance was the last thing on his mind....
Because all Max really wanted was his daughter, and he
knew that marrying Amber was the only way he'd get
close to their child!

Available in December, wherever Harlequin books are sold.